Byker Grove
Odd Ones Out

CW00976735

BYKER GROVE
ODD ONES OUT

James Weir

BBC BOOKS

BYKER GROVE is a Zenith North Production
Published by BBC Books,
a division of BBC Enterprises Limited,
Woodlands, 80 Wood Lane, London W12 0TT
First published 1990
© Hugh Miller 1990
ISBN 0 563 36068 2
Set in Baskerville by Goodfellow & Egan Ltd., Cambridge
Printed and bound in Great Britain by Clays Ltd., St Ives Plc
Cover printed by Clays Ltd., St Ives Plc

CONTENTS

CHAPTER ONE

The alarm went. Gill slid further under the covers, trying to stay asleep, but it wouldn't work. The alarm shattered his dreamscape and dragged him forward into the morning, groaning against the pillow. This wasn't fair. Sleep was freedom, things could be the way he wanted. Waking up was like going to jail.

He opened his eyes and let Tuesday filter in. The first thing he saw was a picture of himself and Julie. His hand closed round the alarm clock. He leaned up on one elbow and heaved the clock across the room.

That didn't help his mood at all. He threw back the clothes and swung his feet over the edge of the bed. For a minute he sat with his elbows on his knees, scratching his head with both hands.

It's just me, now, he thought, precisely as he had thought yesterday morning and the morning before. *There's no us. Just me.*

He forced himself to his feet and shuffled across the room, sidling up to the day rather than facing it. Along the hall he washed, came back and got dressed in his work clothes. He made do with a cup of coffee. On the way out he picked up the letters and thumbed through them. Bills and circulars. Nothing from Julie. He dropped the mail and left.

The traffic noise and the pavement bustle couldn't distract him. Julie throbbed in his head, persistent as toothache and just about as painful. The last words she spoke to him still hurt. That was no surprise, it had only been three nights ago, at the lake. He could hear her clearly, telling him that although she would never forget him, she'd grown out of him. She wanted to do things, she wanted to go to university. If she stayed with him she would never do any of it. Gill admitted to himself now that he'd been flooded with self-pity.

'I'm not good enough for you,' he had whined. 'That's what you're saying.'

She insisted it was the other way round, *she* wasn't good enough for *him*. She was too selfish. She wanted more than he could give her.

Well, he thought grimly, that was true enough.

Near Fletcher's Garage he met up with a couple of other apprentices. They fell into step and ambled along the road together. Near the gate Gill saw his little brush-headed mate, Winston, waiting for him. Come to cheer him up, likely. People just *had* to interfere.

'What're you doing here?' Gill demanded. 'Bunking off school?'

'As if I would,' Winston said.

'As if.'

'I thought I'd bring you some chips at dinner time.'

'No ta.'

'But you like chips, man.'

'I said no,' Gill snapped. 'Just leave us alone, all right?'

'But . . .'

An apprentice called to Gill. It was time to start.

'Look . . .' Gill put up a hand to silence Winston. 'I'll have to go.'

Winston looked stricken. He couldn't handle rejection.

'Yeah, OK,' he sighed. 'I'll see you around.'

He watched, frowning, as Gill trudged off into the yard.

* * *

Maybe it was too early to tell, but Spuggie was sure she wouldn't like long-term fostering.

There was nothing wrong with the foster home. Lou

8

Gallagher was nice; she was as loving, warm and attentive as a real mother. The house was clean and cosy, the food was great and there was a tremendous feeling of safety. No shortage of company, either – Spuggie's brother Fraser was here, so was Speedy and a Vietnamese girl called Joanne. Robert would have been around, too, if it hadn't been for an accident that put him back in dock. As family set-ups went, Spuggie knew this was better than most.

Even so, she wasn't very happy – not as happy as her brother, who appeared to be lapping it up. Living here wasn't the same as living at her own place. This wasn't home, even though home was a high-rise dump, even though her booze-soaked dad had done a disappearing act and her poor mam was so ill and undernourished she'd had to be taken into hospital. Home was more than a place. It wasn't just an address where your letters got sent, where you ate and slept and watched television in between. Home was part of who you were. Home was a million familiar sensations, it was memories and attachments, and Spuggie was missing them all.

But she didn't plan to be a cry-baby about it. This was only temporary, after all. It was only until their mam came out of hospital and was able to look after Fraser and her again. Bearing that in mind, Spuggie kept a bright face as Lou dished out the breakfast. She even smiled a little as Speedy came in, yawning, his shirt tail hanging out and his tie way off centre.

'If anybody's written to Robert today,' Lou said, 'leave it on the hall table. I'll post it when I go out.'

Joanne said she had a letter.

'Me too.' Speedy dropped into a chair at the table. 'I've sent him a photo of Micky Quinn.'

Joanne asked who that was.

'He's only the highest goal scorer in the whole of the football league,' Speedy said.

9

'Never mind that.' Lou put his breakfast in front of him. 'Get a move on. You'll be late again.'

'So? It's only Maths first lesson. I can't do Maths.'

Fraser didn't look convinced.

'Only girls can't do Maths,' he said.

'Really?' Joanne looked indignant. She jerked her head at Speedy. '*He* definitely can't. He gets me to do his Maths homework. He's a wally. Like all boys,' she added.

'So,' Speedy said, 'that makes your precious brother a wally too then?'

'Ge Pao isn't a boy,' Joanne pointed out. 'He's a man. And just you shut up about him, all right?'

When breakfast was over Spuggie went to the bedroom she shared with Joanne and began getting ready for school. A couple of minutes later Joanne breezed in.

'Mam says hurry up or you'll be late.'

'She's not my mam,' Spuggie said. She didn't resent Lou, but she wanted the record kept straight.

'She is mine,' Joanne said.

'Only your foster mam.'

'No, she's my real mam. They adopted me when I was a baby, after I escaped from Vietnam.'

'Why did you have to?'

'Because of the war.'

War was something Spuggie had only seen in films. She couldn't imagine what it must be like, to be afraid to go out in the street in case you got shot or blown up, scared to stay indoors in case you got bombed.

'We lived in Saigon,' Joanne said. 'There was going to be a lot of fighting.'

Spuggie asked what happened to her real mum and dad.

'My mam died. Dad went back to America when the war ended. He didn't care about me. I don't know if he's alive or dead. I've got a brother, though.' Joanne's eyes went distant for a moment. 'He's my only real relative –

10

that I know about.' She picked up a photo from the dressing table and showed it to Spuggie. 'He's called Ge Pao. He's twenty.'

Joanne kissed the picture.

'What's he like?' Spuggie said.

'I've never met him.'

Spuggie felt a tiny pang at her heart.

'He's in Hong Kong. But he writes to me a lot. I've got all his letters.' Joanne pointed to a beautifully decorated box on the dressing table. 'I read them every week.'

'All of them?'

'Every one,' Joanne said huskily. 'I've got hundreds.'

Spuggie felt like hugging her.

* * *

That morning there was more discord than usual in the Dobson house. As they waited for breakfast, Debbie insisted that although her sister Jemma would soon be twelve and old enough to join Byker Grove, she was going to do nothing of the sort. Jemma insisted, just as loudly, that she would if she wanted to. And she wanted to.

'You're not going to join,' Debbie said flatly.

'I am.'

'You're not.'

'It's not up to you,' Jemma said. 'It's up to Geoff. If he says I can, then I can.'

'Aye . . .' Alan Dobson looked wearily at his daughters. 'I've got to put up with the three of you at home. Why shouldn't he suffer?'

'Just 'cos I'm youngest,' Jemma said, glaring at Debbie. 'It's not fair. I always can't do things.'

Kath, their mother, who was working at the stove, said that if Nicola and Debbie both went to the Grove, she couldn't see why Jemma shouldn't.

'I don't see why she has to follow us everywhere, neither,' Debbie said.

For a second she was too perplexed to say any more. She was the victim of an ancient curse, an older sister bedevilled by a younger one who wanted to shadow her all over the place.

'There's Wallsend and Saint Anthony's and Hadrian Road,' she said. 'Their clubs are all right.'

'So why don't you go to them if they're so brilliant?' Jemma demanded.

Nicola came into the kitchen and sat down.

'Bacon, Nicola?' Kath asked.

Nicola looked appalled.

'You know I don't eat that stuff.'

Since becoming aware of mankind's barbaric treatment of the environment, Nicola had turned sympathetic towards nature in general and edible creatures in particular.

'You can't go to school on an apple,' Kath complained. 'You're getting anorexic.'

'Mam, I am not getting anorexic. I'm just not into eating animals, all right?'

'Bacon's not an animal,' Jemma piped up.

'It was, stupid,' Debbie said. 'It was once a pig.'

'All right you two,' Kath warned, 'that's quite enough.' She glanced at the door, then lowering her voice, she said, 'I want a word with you all before your gran comes down.'

'What about?' Nicola said. 'She's not poorly again, is she?'

'No, she's fine. It's just that –'

Kath broke off as Mary O'Malley, the girls' grandmother, came into the kitchen. The old woman blinked suspiciously at the abrupt silence.

'What are you lot talking about?' She waited, looking at them each in turn. 'Well?'

'Bacon, Gran,' Jemma said.

'Good.' Mrs O'Malley sat down, beaming. 'Let's be having some, then.'

When breakfast was over and the girls were preparing to leave for school, their gran announced she was off down to the butcher's before he got busy.

'A nice bit of breast of lamb, if he's got it,' she said. 'And a bag of carrots for Bugs Bunny,' she added, nodding at Nicola. 'You need fattening up, you do.'

Nicola pretended not to hear. When Gran had gone, Kath beckoned the girls round her.

'Right,' she said, 'the thing is, you know it's her seventieth birthday next week? Your dad and me want to make her a bit of a do.'

'Who're you asking?' Nicola said.

'Your Auntie Doris and Uncle Phil, some of the neighbours, her pals from the Day Centre . . .'

'We don't have to come, do we?' Debbie said, scowling.

'Of course you do,' her dad said.

'They're all dead ancient.'

Alan told her she would be there, so she could stop pulling faces. They would all be there. Kath pointed out it was to be a surprise, so nobody had to say a word. Nicola couldn't see how they would manage to keep it a secret.

'Your dad'll get Geoff to make sure she's needed at the Grove,' Kath said. 'Then when everybody's here, we'll find some excuse to fetch her back.'

Jemma listened to the explanation with a serious, thoughtful face.

'That's being crafty,' she said.

'You're right,' her dad said. 'It is.'

Jemma sniffed.

'When I'm crafty, you always tell me off. It's not fair.'

* * *

At dinner time, letting himself be carried through the school gates on a bobbing current of other kids, Speedy heard his name called. He stopped and looked round. When he saw who it was he shut his eyes a moment and looked again. No mistake. It was Jan, the Danish lad Donna Bell had fallen for, before she discovered he had a serious girlfriend back in Copenhagen. He had a beautiful blonde girl with him now. Speedy wondered if that was her. He walked back along the pavement, smiling.

'It is me, remember?' Jan said.

'Oh yes,' Speedy nodded. 'Donna's boyfriend – oop! Sorry!'

Jan smiled broadly.

'How are you? How is everybody at the Grove?'

'They're OK.'

'And how's Donna?'

'Er . . . she's OK.' Speedy had a flashing memory of Donna, the way she fell apart when she discovered Jan wouldn't be the great love of her life after all. 'What are you doing here? Have you come back?'

'No,' Jan said, 'Kirsten and I are just on a short visit. Now I am taking her to meet my landlady, who was so kind to me when I was here. Kirsten, this is my friend Speedy.'

She gave Speedy a dazzling smile.

'Pleased to meet you,' he said, swallowing.

Jan suggested they go for a coffee together.

'Well . . .' Speedy was tempted. 'I was just going for a pastie, but . . . yeah. 'Course. Great.' He tried to imagine what Donna would do if she knew Jan was back in town. He would make sure she found out. 'So long as I'm back for half-one,' he said, smiling shyly at Kirsten. 'It's games.'

* * *

14

Marylin Charlton, known to all as Charlie, was gazing dreamily into the window of a town-centre record shop when PJ came along. He stood beside her for a moment, looking in the window, mimicking the expression she'd had before she spotted him.

'Imagining yours is in there, are you?' he said.

'Don't be daft.'

Charlie had hopes for her forthcoming record, high hopes at that, but she was superstitious about admitting it.

'Why's it daft?' PJ demanded. 'If your record's any good you could be another Kylie. She came out of nowhere at the start. They all did. Madonna, Paula Abdul, Yazz – all ordinary girls, once.'

'I hate it when people send me up,' Charlie said, not sure if he was.

'There's nothing wrong in wanting to be famous, girl.' For a teenager, PJ could sound disarmingly seasoned. '*I* definitely intend to be. I'm going to walk in places and they'll turn round and say, "You know who that is? That is PJ Jenkins!" '

'Can you sing?'

'Nah. But nor can old Tel Wogan. We've got the gift of the gab, us. This record of yours, reckon it's a contender?'

'Steve thinks so.'

'He's got the business sussed, then?'

'Of course he has.' Charlie realised she'd sounded defensive. 'He's got his own record company.'

PJ nodded, looking more interested now.

'What was the name again? Steve what?'

'Rettega,' Charlie said. 'Polythene Records. He's got this big studio in Corporation Street. He's sort of like a Geordie Richard Branson.'

A short time later, and further across town, Fraser Campbell cycled past Mrs O'Malley on her way to work at Byker Grove. He called out, then got off his bike and waited for her. She came towards him smiling.

'How are you both settling in?' she said, drawing level.

'Well . . .' Fraser shrugged. 'Spuggie doesn't say much.'

'Give her time, pet. How about you?'

'It's great,' he said, feeling that was inadequate. 'Great' hardly covered it. For the first time in his life he was a member of a safe, united, *happy* family. 'It's 'specially great being with Speedy.'

'He's a nice lad,' Mary O'Malley said. 'So you're happy, then?'

'Apart from Mam still being in hospital.'

There was always a sadness somewhere. Fraser was still only young but he knew that was true. Always a pain to distract you from the sweetest things. No silver lining without a cloud . . .

'She'll be out eventually,' Mrs O'Malley said. 'Now's your chance to enjoy being young for a bit. Take it from me, it goes too quick.'

At the Grove Fraser parked his bike and they walked into the house together. In the hallway Mrs O'Malley stopped, looked both ways, then leaned close.

'I'll tell you a secret,' she said in a low voice. 'It's my birthday next week. Know how old I'll be?'

'No,' Fraser said, hoping she wouldn't ask him to guess.

'Seventy,' she whispered. 'But keep it under your hat. I don't want them all knowing.'

They moved on, passing PJ who was using the telephone. As they went by he was asking for the number of Polythene Records.

'Are you having a party?' Fraser said.

Mary shook her head, making a face.

'When you get to my age, pet, you don't want a lot of fuss.'

Behind them PJ punched in the number Directory Enquiries had given him. He waited, letting it ring out. After a minute, getting no response, he put the receiver back on the hook.

In the big main room Charlie was bringing Donna and Nicola up to date on Robert's progress in hospital. Nicola wanted to know how much longer he would be in.

'Few weeks,' Charlie said, 'they don't really know. I made him laugh when I 'phoned him, though. I was telling him about me stylist –'

'Your what?' Donna said.

'Stylist. Steve says he's going to get me one.'

'Yeah, well,' Donna said archly. 'You could certainly use a bit of style.'

'That's not what it's for,' Charlie said. 'It's somebody who creates an image for you. A total look for when you're doing videos and PAs. Them's personal appearances.'

'I know what PAs are,' Donna snapped. 'When I'm a top model I'll be doing them all the time.'

Speedy came in. The instant he saw Donna he came across.

'I saw an old boyfriend of yours today,' he said.

'Oh, yes?' Donna affected faint interest. 'Which one?'

'Jan.'

The name fell like a small explosion on Donna's ears, but she managed to hang on to her cool.

'Jan? You can't have. He's in Denmark.'

'He's not,' Speedy said. 'He's in Newcastle. He's showing a girlfriend round. Her name's Kirsten. They've just got engaged.'

'That's nice,' Donna said, her teeth scarcely parting.

'She loved Bamburgh, 'specially the castle. And he's taking her to Cragside tomorrow.'

Donna blinked.

'Where?'

'Cragside. He said he wanted to show her all the special places he went while he was here. He said to send you his regards.'

'That was sweet of him.'

Speedy suddenly spotted a friend, Gozo, and moved away. Nicola turned to Donna.

'Don't you mind?' she said.

'Why should I?' Donna's mouth sounded dry. 'He's yesterday's news.'

Outside, meanwhile, little Winston was crouched over the competition leeks, furtively tipping liquid fertiliser on them. A hand landed heavily on his shoulder and he nearly dropped the bottle.

'Got you!'

Winston looked up and saw Alan Dobson. Alan had supervised the growing of the leeks from the time it was decided Byker Grove would enter the competition. Geoff Keegan stood behind Alan.

'What you been doing, Winston?' Geoff demanded.

Alan seized the bottle and stared at the label.

'Only feeding them up to their eyebrows,' he said. 'I told you something was going on!'

'I was only trying to help,' Winston complained.

Geoff was eyeing the leeks. They certainly looked sturdy.

'Isn't it good they're a bit on the large side?' he asked Alan.

'Good? It's a flaming disaster.'

Debbie came round the corner.

'Hiya, Dad,' she said, taking in the little tableau. 'What's a flaming disaster?'

'Them,' Alan barked, pointing at the leeks. 'And watch your language, young lady.' He stared at the leeks again, groaning. 'They've only peaked, grown themselves out of their class. They're blimmin' freaks.'

Speedy and Gozo came past. Speedy took in Alan's glum expression, then Geoff's.

'What's up?'

'We've got freak peaked leeks,' Debbie said.

'Thanks to your friend here,' Alan said grimly, 'who's fed them too much stuff.'

Speedy looked at the leeks. He couldn't see anything wrong with them, beyond the fact they were whoppers.

'We can still go in for the competition though, can't we?'

'Haway,' Alan said, shaking his head. 'We'd be laughed out of the show. They're monsters. You've just let Denton Burn walk away with it.'

That information changed everything. Speedy's face began to churn. In the space of seconds it had turned livid.

'Winston!' he roared. 'You total pillock!' He looked around. 'Where is he?'

As Speedy spoke, Winston was streaking towards the gate.

* * *

Ronnie, the foreman at Fletcher's Garage, was watching Gill work on a car engine. It was a fussy job – a gasket replacement and a new oil filter to be fitted – and today Gill's concentration wasn't up to speed. Eventually Ronnie came across the workshop.

'How much longer you going to be with that, Gillespie?'

Gill straightened, wiping his hand on his overalls.

'Dunno,' he said.

'You should have finished it over an hour ago. You want to buck your ideas up, sonny. It's a garage we're running here, not a play group.'

Ronnie turned and stumped away. Gill looked around

19

for a Stillson wrench, wondering if the foreman knew that only a couple more words would have won him a sore chin.

There was no sign of a wrench, even though there had been one lying on the oil drum by the car ten minutes ago. People just took tools without asking. Gill wandered out to the yard to look for another one. Rummaging around near the fence, he looked up and saw Winston standing on the other side.

'Talk about blimmin' bad pennies,' Gill grunted.

'I thought I'd hang around till you finish,' Winston said, trying to sound bright.

'Haven't you got nowhere else to go?'

'No. We could go somewhere later, if you like.'

'You're not getting us back at that Grove. No way.'

'Me neither,' Winston said. 'It's gone a right dump. But we could go down the Metrocentre. Or bowling. Or Walker Wheels, it was ace that time we went with Brad . . .'

'Look . . .' Gill had been drumming his fingers on the fence. He stood back now, glaring at Winston. 'You just won't get it, will you? That was kids' stuff. I'm not a kid any more.'

Winston stared back bleakly.

'She ain't never coming back, you know,' he said.

Gill took a deep, careful breath.

'Thanks for telling us.'

'So forget her, man. She ain't worth it. I never rated her much anyway. Stuck up cow.'

'Did I ask you?' Gill demanded, so loud it made Winston jump. 'Did I blimmin' ask you, you miserable little runt? Now do us both a favour and bog off, all right? And this time don't bother coming back!'

The foreman had been watching from the workshop door. He took a step forward and yelled for Gill to get inside.

Gill turned and walked back to the workshop, leaving Winston feeling as if he had been thumped.

* * *

In the main room at the Grove Debbie was attempting, yet again, to satisfy her curiosity. She had cornered a reluctant Spuggie.

'Speedy says the lady at your place says to call her Lou. What's it short for? Lavatory?'

'Louise,' Spuggie said. 'Louise and Mick.'

'I'd get a clout if I called me mam and dad Alan and Kath.' Debbie was instantly distracted as PJ walked into the room. 'Don't you think he's sort of cute?' she murmured. 'I do.'

'I've more important things to think about than stupid boys,' Spuggie said, frowning severely as her brother stepped up to PJ and spoke to him.

'Hey, PJ, m'man,' Fraser said. 'How do you fancy strutting your DJ stuff again?'

PJ stared at him aghast.

'Don't even try it, man,' he said. 'Ain't your style. Leave cool to us naturals.'

'OK, OK. But will you do it?'

'Just lead me to the deck. Where's the gig?'

'Here,' Fraser said. 'Next week.'

'Great!' PJ's face lit up. 'I was getting withdrawal symptoms.'

Fraser dropped his voice and explained.

'It's a birthday party surprise for her.'

'I like it. Who's the lucky chick, then? Nicola? Charlie? Can't be Donna, she's just had hers . . .'

'It's Mary.'

'Mary who?'

'Mary O'Malley.' Fraser could see the name rang no bell with PJ. 'Gran. She's done a lot for me and Spug.'

21

PJ looked mildly shocked.

'You want ol' PJ to DJ a rave-up for Mrs O'Malley? You are *joking*, man!' He peered at Fraser's sombre face. 'You're not joking!'

Over in the corner Donna was doing her best to demoralise Charlie.

'Even if you do scrape into the bottom of the charts,' she said, 'you'll be a one-hit wonder.'

'Why will she?' Nicola demanded.

'Because most of 'em are. Famous for a week then they sink without trace. Back to the supermarket checkout.'

Charlie turned to Nicola.

'She is seriously depressing, your friend.'

'Take no notice,' Nicola said. 'I never do.'

Donna went to get drinks at the snack bar.

'Why is it,' Charlie asked, 'nobody else is allowed to have good things happen to them, only Donna Bell?'

'It's when good things make you the centre of attention,' Nicola explained. 'She has to be that.'

'Heaven knows what she'll be like when me record actually comes out.'

'When is that, anyway?'

'I'll know as soon as I speak to Steve. But it can't be long.'

'Well,' Nicola said, spreading her hands, 'we'll just have to hope madam gets to be a top model soon. No, on second thoughts, that'd be even worse.' She cocked her head at Charlie. 'Would you really like to be a big star?'

'Of course. Wouldn't everybody?'

Donna came back. As usual her hearing had arrived ahead of her.

'Everybody what?' she said, putting down the drinks.

'I wouldn't,' Nicola said, ignoring Donna. 'Oh, I'd like the dosh, all right. Buy me mam and dad a decent house and stuff. Ship our Debbie and Jemma to Australia. But

I wouldn't like it that people were fawning round me all the time. Just 'cos of who I was.'

'You'd still have your real friends,' Charlie said.

Nicola shrugged.

'How would you know, though? How would you know if they like you and not just what they can get out of you?'

'Who'd want to do that?' Donna said, wide-eyed, looking from one to the other.

In the office Geoff was talking to Mrs O'Malley about Duncan, who hadn't been near the Grove since Geoff uncovered him as the one who had been stealing money.

'He's not been in for the past week,' Geoff said. 'Probably too ashamed.'

'He's no villain, isn't little Duncan. They're a beggar, them machines.' Duncan had got himself addicted to the arcade machines at the bowling alley and had been stealing to finance his habit. 'If grown men get hooked, you can see why a lad might.'

'I had a word with PC Grant,' Geoff said. 'They'll not take any further action so long as I'm happy to deal with it internally — like refunding the money myself!' Geoff craned his neck, seeing Spuggie heading for the door. 'Off home already, Spug?'

She paused.

'It's not home,' she said, her face very serious. 'It's just a place we're stopping till our mam gets better.'

Geoff smiled as Spuggie left.

'I know the Gallaghers,' he said. 'They're a good couple. And I'll wager her and Fraser haven't eaten as well in the whole of their lives.'

It was almost half an hour later that Joanne came out of the Gallaghers' house and came across to the park where Spuggie was sitting.

'What are you sitting here for?'

'Just felt like it,' Spuggie said.

Joanne nodded.

'It's nice living across the road from a park.'

'It's all right.'

Joanne was quiet for a minute, listening to the trees.

'Shall I tell you something?' she said.

'If you want.'

'I never knew I had a brother till I was thirteen.'

Spuggie looked at her.

'How come?'

'We got separated. I was brought over to England by this charity organisation. When he got put in this camp, he tracked me down. It was the best moment in my whole life when I got his first letter. I'll show it you if you like. Come on.'

The girls went back to the house. In the bedroom Joanne pulled her box out from under her bed. She opened it and carefully undid one of the ribbon-tied packets of letters.

'So where is he now?' Spuggie said.

'Still in the camp. He was one of the Boat People. He's been trying to come over here for ages, but it's very hard to get permission.'

'I'm sorry,' Spuggie said, meaning it.

'Yeah, well, you should be,' Joanne murmured, making Spuggie stare at her. 'Feeling sorry for yourself the whole time. At least your mam'll be home one day. And you've got a dad, even if you don't know where he is.'

Spuggie supposed she deserved that reminder. She frowned at the carpet for a minute, recalling what Joanne had told her earlier.

'I thought you said Mr and Mrs Gallagher were your mum and dad now?'

'They are. They've been very good to me and I love them. But just sometimes I can't help wishing . . .'

Spuggie nodded. She believed she understood.

Without planning to, she leaned across and gently squeezed Joanne's shoulder.

* * *

Early the following evening Debbie Dobson pounced on PJ as he walked up the drive to the Grove.

'Hiya,' she chirruped at him. 'Can I ask you something?'

'Go on.'

'Have you got a girlfriend?'

'Hundreds.'

'Oh. I've not got a boyfriend. Well, not yet.'

PJ shook his head sadly.

'On the shelf at twelve. Mega tragic, kid.'

'I'm not twelve,' Debbie pointed out, 'I'm thirteen.' She fluttered her eyelids in a way she believed was provocative. 'I don't think two years between people is too much, do you?'

'Depends which two people.'

'Yes, that's what I thought.'

As Debbie confidently linked her arm with his, PJ began to understand he had a problem.

They went into the house arm in arm, but PJ managed to shake loose as they entered the main room. He made straight for Charlie and asked her, without preamble, how he could get in touch with the bloke who was doing her record.

Debbie had tagged along and was taking a keen interest.

'What do you want him for?' she asked.

'Debbie, butt out, eh?'

'What do you want him for?' Charlie said.

'Oh . . .' PJ made an offhand gesture. 'I thought if he's such a hot shot he might have a niche for a bright young lad in his organisation.'

Charlie looked uncomfortable about this.

'You're not to pester him,' she said. 'He's a busy man.'

'I only want to ask if he's got any part-time jobs going. What's wrong with that? I don't mind starting as a gofer.'

'Just don't embarrass us, that's all,' Charlie insisted.

'I'd have to find him first.'

'What do you mean?'

PJ said he had rung Polythene Records and there was no reply. Charlie didn't find that surprising – Steve went out a lot. She said he was probably at the studio. But PJ had tried there, too, and they hadn't a clue where Steve was. Charlie wouldn't buy that; the company was owned by Steve, after all.

'Nope,' PJ said. 'The guy there said it's just a facilities place, lots of people use it. Your guy's just one of them.'

Charlie's faith was a blockhouse. She shrugged and told PJ he had obviously got it wrong.

'Well,' he said, 'when you do make contact, put in a word for us, eh?'

Charlie said she would think about it. PJ sloped off to the snack bar with Debbie following. Winston slunk in through the door and stood there. The place became quieter. Winston smiled at Charlie.

'Good luck with your record,' he said.

'Trust PJ for cheek,' Charlie said to Nicola. 'Trying to muscle in on the act.'

Winston cleared his throat.

'When did you say it was coming out?' he said.

'Don't suppose it'll do any harm,' Nicola told Charlie. She looked at her watch. 'I wonder where Donna is?'

Winston turned to Nicola.

'You still a vegetarian? Must be funny, not eating meat.'

'Probably having her hair dyed purple,' Charlie said.

'Or a diamond stud in her nose,' Nicola said, giggling.

Winston felt like the invisible man. He turned and saw Fraser come in with Speedy. They crossed the room and joined PJ, who was still being shadowed by Debbie. Winston went across, smiled cordially at the assembled company and enquired if anyone fancied a game of ping-pong.

Fraser asked Speedy if he was coming to the party on Thursday.

'You bet,' Speedy said. 'What party?'

'All will be revealed in due course,' PJ told him. 'Just be there, right?'

'Can anybody come?' Winston asked.

'Six o'clock on the button,' Fraser told Speedy.

'And bring your Elvis tape,' PJ added.

Debbie stared at PJ.

'Elvis?' she said. 'Who's Elvis?'

'All right!' Winston yelled to the room at large. 'I'm sorry! I didn't mean to ruin the rotten leeks. I was only trying to help. I wanted us to blimmin' win, didn't I? How was I to know they'd grow into something from outer space?'

He scanned the room. There wasn't a trace of forgiveness to be found. He shrugged and walked out, trying his hardest to swagger.

* * *

Gill spooned coffee into a mug. He picked up the kettle and shook it. Empty. He would have to fill it from the tap down the hall. He opened the door and found Winston standing there.

'Do you never give up?'

Winston's expression was somewhere between hang-dog and pleading.

'I just wanted to say sorry for putting you on the spot yesterday, Gill. Did he give you any hassle, that bloke?'

27

'Ronnie? He's a nerd.'

Winston wet his lips nervously.

'Look, man, what I said about the Duchess . . . about Julie . . . I didn't mean it. I know you were dead cut up . . .'

'Just drop it,' Gill said.

'You'll be OK, though. There's plenty of other fish in the sea. Good old Geordie ones. And you've still got me.' A note of panicky brightness entered Winston's voice. 'Gill and Win, the old team, right?'

Gill stared at him coldly.

'History, sunshine,' he said. 'Like me and the Duchess. All history.'

Winston's brightness disintegrated. He swallowed hard. Twice.

'You mean . . . you don't want to be mates any more?'

Gill nodded curtly.

'Got it in one.'

He slammed down the kettle and strode out. A moment later the outside door banged shut. Winston stood alone in the echoing room, bewildered. He picked up a photograph of Julie and stared at it.

'It's all your fault,' he hissed. 'All your blimmin' fault.'

* * *

Gill left the house and kept walking, not caring where he went. His awareness of the world outside himself – the street, buildings, the traffic and other people – was dulled by the bruising chaos inside. His thoughts were an uncontrolled jumble of images, reeking with regret. Above all else he wanted peace. He wanted the power to forget, and if he couldn't have that he wanted indifference, he wanted to lose the ability to care.

He set his jaw, forcing himself to look at things, to take stock. He was on a main road with heavy traffic.

The pavement was thick with people coming and going, talking and smiling. Laughing.

Laughter for Gill was a series of memories tied to his days with Julie. The best laughter he could remember, the *only* laughter, came from glorious moments of daftness when all that mattered was to enjoy each other and the time they shared.

He jerked his mind away from all that. To hell with Julie. To *hell* with her and the memories of her. Memory was the country of dead times. It was no place for the living to dwell.

His footsteps slowed as a beautiful sports car pulled up at the kerbside ten yards ahead. A young couple got out. They linked arms as they moved away. The pain of their closeness was a clamp on Gill's chest. He looked away.

His steps got slower still as his attention wandered back to what first held it. The car. It was a beauty. A classic. As he drew close he saw the keys, still in the ignition.

You have to stick your neck out sometimes. He had said that to Julie once, back at the beginning.

He looked along the street, first behind him, then in front.

One, two . . . *three*!

His body jackknifed as his hand shot out and opened the door. In a flash he was sliding across the passenger seat and in behind the wheel. The door shut as he fired the engine and engaged the gear. He felt the jolt on his back as the car surged forward, into the traffic, the speed climbing in response to the pressure of his foot on the pedal.

No wonder they called it joy-riding. It was liberation, purest glee, rushing between the other cars on a wave of impulse that he *knew* could carry him as long and as far as he wanted to go. The faster he went the smaller the pain became. Speed was anaesthetic.

He twisted the wheel and charged past two wallies in

shiny limos, shock-faced boss-types with ties and white shirts, scared witless by the free spirit tearing on ahead of them, wobbling their stately vehicles with his side-wash. Gill lowered his toe a fraction on the pedal. He was in the middle of the road now, dominating it. He had a vague notion he was heading south. South it was, then. He was eating up tarmac but there was plenty of it. The engine roared and filled his head with the music of synchronised pistons, the song of escape.

He heard a whining note and looked in the mirror. Maybe fifteen yards behind he saw a police car. His heart swelled as he slammed down his foot and gripped the wheel tighter, aiming the car like a missile, swinging into an impossible corner and making it, taking the whole width of the road to regain control of the car.

He looked in the mirror again. The police car was staying with him. He'd heard about the souped-up engines in those things. Ahead the road was dead straight with hardly any traffic. Gill put his foot right down to the floor and as the engine screamed he watched for a turning, any turn-off at all.

One appeared on the left, just up ahead. He was on top of it incredibly fast. He tugged on the wheel, had to hang on with both hands as it fought him. The car heeled over and screeched into the bend, leaving two elegant curves of rubber on the road as he straightened and accelerated along a side street.

He sighted a lay-by. The mirror showed no police car but he could hear it not far away. Dropping down through the gears he tooled the car towards the lay-by, braked and jumped out.

He was running an instant after his feet hit the pavement. He heard the squad car coming, the siren getting louder, a threat, the enemy of freedom. By the time the police drew up beside the sports car, Gill was nowhere in sight.

Twenty minutes later he got to his room at the squat and slammed the door shut behind him. He was seething with frustrated anger. Standing in the middle of the floor, panting, his chest burning, he gazed around at the posters Julie had given him. He stared at all the other little signs and symbols of the time when she had been there, when she had *wanted* to be there. Before she rejected him.

In a sudden rage Gill tore down the posters, ripping them to shreds. He snatched up the pot plant and flung it in the bin. The carved bird soared through the window and smashed to fragments on the road outside. He gathered up the photographs of himself and Julie and began tearing them to bits, whining in his throat as the pieces flew around him, sounding like an animal unspeakably hurt.

CHAPTER TWO

Early on Monday evening Nicola called at the Byker
Arms for Donna. It was a set routine; Nicola called for
Donna, waited while Donna finished dolling herself up,
then they went off together to the Grove. But tonight
Donna came to the door and announced she wasn't
going.

'Why not? If it's because of Charlie . . . '

'It's not.'

Nicola wasn't convinced. She tried to explain that
Donna had nothing to be jealous of. Charlie was a nice girl.
She was excited about her record coming out, but she
didn't swank about it or ram it down anybody's throat.

'Look,' Donna said, 'I'm not bothered about her
stupid little record, and I'm not bothered about her.'

'So what is it then? Something's bugging you.'

Donna said she was just fed up. To counter that,
Nicola asked her if she would fancy coming to a party on
Thursday. Donna looked a shade brighter, until Nicola
explained it was her gran's party.

'Oh, do us a favour!'

'She's going to be seventy,' Nicola said. 'We've asked
all her friends.'

'Sounds wild. What'll they be playing? Spin the bath-
chair and pensioner's knock?'

'Will you come?' Nicola put on her beseeching face.
'At least it'll be someone for me to talk to.'

'I'll think about it,' Donna said coolly, and without
another word she went back inside.

At roughly the same time as Nicola walked away from
the Byker Arms, Brad, the photography instructor and
so much else, was arriving at the Grove in his little sports
car. As he turned off the engine he caught sight of
Nicola's sister Jemma. She was crying.

'What's to do?' he said as she approached the car.

'It's Rosie,' Jemma said. 'The rag-and-bone man's horse.' She took a deep shuddering breath. 'She's going to the knacker's yard.'

Brad told her to get in and tell him all about it. He held open the door and she clambered in beside him. Between sniffles she delivered her story.

It appeared that earlier that evening Jemma's dad, Alan, and Ted Boneo, the rag-and-bone man, had brought an old iron bath round to the Dobson house. It had been pulled there on the cart by Ted's old mare Rosie. To hear Jemma tell it, Rosie was the finest horse ever to go between shafts, a powerful yet soft-eyed creature, a flawless blend of elegance, strength, character and gentility. Jemma had stood stroking the beast's head while her dad had explained to Ted how he would plug the holes in the bathtub, fill it with water and have himself a cracking little water garden.

It was later, Jemma told Brad, just before Ted left, that he'd said Rosie would soon be off to the knacker's yard.

Brad agreed it didn't sound as if there was much doubt about Rosie's future, but he thought they should check with Ted Boneo anyway, just to be sure Jemma hadn't got the story wrong.

'Fasten your seat belt, love.'

Brad drove over to the junk yard where, standing among rusting mounds of Newcastle's throw-outs and cast-offs, Ted Boneo confirmed that Rosie would soon be visiting the knacker's yard.

'The young un's got it right,' he said. 'It's a shame, but there's nothing else for it.'

Jemma was distraught. She turned big appealing eyes to Brad.

'The knacker's yard means she's going to be killed, doesn't it?'

'I'm afraid it does, pet,' Brad said.

'I'm retiring, see,' Ted said. 'Going to live with me daughter in Durham. And there's no place there for old Rosie.'

'She's going to die,' Jemma wailed, 'and it's not even her fault. It's not fair. Oh, Brad, can't you do anything?'

Brad stared across at the old horse, chomping gently at the oats in her nose bag. There must be *something* he could do, he supposed. Anything could be changed if you wanted change badly enough. That's what his grannie had led him to believe, anyway.

'Let's go and see Geoff,' he said, prodding the red-eyed Jemma gently towards the car.

* * *

Geoff had finally sent for little Duncan. The lad sat now in the office at the Grove, silent and fearful as Geoff closed the door to give them privacy. Duncan was particularly small and he looked even smaller as Geoff's sizeable bulk swept past him and dropped into the chair behind the desk.

Geoff folded his hands on the desktop and looked squarely at Duncan.

'You're good with figures, they tell me.'

Duncan hadn't been sure what to expect, but it certainly wasn't anything like this.

'Yes,' he said, looking down at his tangled fingers. 'But . . .'

'Right,' Geoff said briskly, 'so here's the plan. I'm going to put you in charge of the Grove's petty cash.'

Duncan stared at him.

'*What?*'

Geoff pushed an open ledger across the desk.

'There's the book. That's the current balance, here's the float.'

Duncan looked at the figures. They simply danced in front of his eyes. He looked at Geoff again.

'I don't get it. I took money from you!'

Geoff nodded amiably.

'It's an old principle, son. Set a thief to catch a thief. Only in this case, they're both you. If we're so much as a penny piece short, who's going to get fingered?'

'I am,' Duncan said.

'Yes! You are!' Geoff sat back in his chair. 'Besides, I also happen to think you'll be good at it. Better than me, any road.' He shook his head at the book. 'Never can get it to balance.'

There was a good deal Duncan could have said, if he'd had the courage and the words. As it was, tongue-tied and grateful, he drew the book towards him, closed it and stood up.

'Thanks, Geoff.'

'Hey . . . ' Geoff stopped him as he opened the door. 'Any time you're tempted to go on one of those machines, you're to 'phone me. Right?'

'Right,' Duncan frowned. 'Why?'

'I'll twirl round,' Geoff said, 'put me Y-fronts over me tights and before you can so much as stick a coin in the slot, SuperGeoff will be there to stop you.' He winked. 'Right?'

Later, making his customary evening tour of the Grove, Geoff was approached in the main room by Fraser and PJ. Fraser, as spokesman, asked if he and PJ could put on a party at the Grove on Thursday.

'What's it for?'

'Just somebody special . . . '

Brad appeared beside Geoff. Jemma was with him. Her eyes were still red. Debbie, who never missed anything, didn't miss this. She came and stood nearby.

'Geoff,' Brad said, cutting in on Fraser, 'Jemma wants to ask you something.'

'If it's can she join the Grove,' Debbie yelped, 'tell her no.'

'It's not, cleverclogs,' Jemma said. 'But if it was, he said I could when I'm twelve.'

'Well, you're not,' Debbie said.

'Almost,' Jemma reminded her.

'Aw, say she can't come, Geoff, go on . . .'

'Only there's this poor old horse,' Jemma said, addressing Geoff now, 'and it's going to be put down just because there's nowhere for it to go . . .'

'*Almost* isn't twelve,' Debbie interrupted.

'We can't tell you because it's a surprise,' Fraser said, trying to get Geoff's attention again.

'I was thinking,' Brad said, 'we've plenty of grass here . . .'

'*Please*, Geoff,' Debbie wailed.

'Geoff,' Jemma cried, '*please* . . .'

Geoff took one defensive step backwards.

'No!' he snapped. He turned to Fraser and PJ. 'And no to you.' He looked at Debbie. 'And no to you. And no to anybody else, including you. Whatever you want, the answer's no.'

He turned and marched off. Debbie led Jemma away.

Alison had appeared halfway through the muddled exchange and now she was giving Brad an amused look. She came forward as the disgruntled Fraser and PJ wandered off.

'What's biting Geoff?' Brad said.

Alison shrugged. She was Geoff's longest-serving assistant, but there were still times when he puzzled her.

'I don't know. But it's not some poor old homeless horse.'

She kept up the amused, slightly mocking expression, making Brad wonder if it was some kind of spite, an attempt to punish him for just being around and undermining her loyalty to Mike, the man she lived with. Brad didn't think he was flattering himself; he knew Alison was powerfully attracted to him, whether she could admit it or not.

'I just want it to have somewhere to spend its last days in peace,' Brad said. 'What's wrong with that?'

'Nothing,' Alison drawled. 'It's very touching.'

'Never mind laughing, madam,' he said stiffly. 'How would you like it if they took you out to be shot once you were too old to work?'

'I'm not laughing, Brad,' she lied, barely containing herself. 'I think it's terrific you're so concerned. And for a horse you don't even know.'

'I'm wasting my time, anyway,' Brad sighed. 'You heard what the guv'nor said. Another one with a heart of stone.'

Fraser and PJ had withdrawn to the games room. PJ had been looking pretty relieved since Geoff turned down their request to hold a party at the Grove. Fraser told him he needn't look so chuffed.

'I'm not,' PJ swore. 'Honest. Only you have to admit, it wouldn't exactly do a load for my image, deejaying for a bunch of old wrinklies.'

Fraser was about to argue with that when Geoff came in, looking embarrassed. He shuffled over to them.

'Er, lads. Look, I'm sorry I lost my rag. I just wanted to say it'll be OK for Thursday.'

'Hey, great, man!' Fraser yelled, delighted.

'Yeah, brilliant,' PJ muttered.

Geoff rubbed his chin, looking from one to the other, weighing their reliability.

'I'm trusting you, mind,' he said. 'This do had better be in a worthwhile cause. Because if it turns out to be another of your scatty ideas like the radio station . . .'

'It's not, Geoff,' Fraser said. 'Honest.' He grabbed PJ's arm. 'Come on.'

'Where?'

Under his breath, Fraser explained they had to make sure Mary O'Malley would come to the party. At the door Fraser turned.

'Geoff,' he called. 'You're invited, too.'

'Thanks a bunch,' Geoff grunted as they dashed out.

Mrs O'Malley was in the hallway with little Duncan. He was holding the ledger open in front of her.

'Stock control!' he said triumphantly, his eyes bright with the inner light of the converted. 'This column's for cakes and biscuits. This one's for sandwiches. This one's for cold drinks . . . '

'Never had to put 'em separate before,' Mary said. 'Anything we sell in the snack bar, we just total it up at the end of the day and jot it down.'

'Yes, well, this is the new system,' Duncan said patiently. 'Much more efficient.'

'Much more fiddly, far as I can see. I mean, if I've got to enter every bag of crisps . . . ' Mary looked up as Fraser and PJ approached. 'You've not come to tell me I've got to count every peanut before I sell 'em, I hope?'

'No,' Fraser said, frowning. 'But there is a little favour we'd like you to do for us.'

'Go on.'

'We're having a bit of a party on Thursday night and we wondered if you'd help us serve the grub.'

Mrs O'Malley considered that.

'Who's making it, then?'

'We are,' Fraser said. 'Geoff says it can come out of the petty cash.'

Duncan bristled.

'I've not been informed about this,' he snapped.

'Well you're being informed now,' Fraser told him. He turned to Mary again. 'Can you do it? We'd need you here by half-past six.'

Mary began to take on the look of someone smelling a rat.

'You don't need me here just to help serve a few sandwiches.'

'Yes, we do,' Fraser said bravely, his face stiff with conviction.

'What's it in aid of, anyway?' Mary wanted to know.

'Somebody we think deserves a fuss making of her.'

Mary frowned for a minute, then suddenly her face cleared.

'Spuggie!' she cried. 'It's for Spuggie, isn't it? I know she's been a bit down lately, poor little mite.' She beamed at Fraser and PJ. 'Yes, of course I'll help, if it's for her. It'll be my pleasure.'

* * *

Nicola was in her bedroom when she heard the doorbell ring. She opened the window and looked out. Donna was on the doorstep.

'I thought you said you weren't going to the Grove,' Nicola said.

'I'm not. But I've got to talk to you.'

'Go on then.'

'Not here,' Donna said, looking wounded.

Nicola told her to come up – the key was on a string through the letterbox. Donna fished it out, unlocked the door and let herself in. She made sure the door was locked again and the key back through the letter slot before she went up the stairs. Nicola met her on the landing and led the way into her bedroom.

'So what's up? Something's been bugging you.'

Donna sat on the end of the bed, looking pale and serious.

'I think I'm pregnant,' she said.

Nicola's face ran through a variety of expressions, all of them surprised.

'What?'

'I'm late,' Donna hissed.

'How late?'

'Few days.'

Nicola's tension began to relax.

'That's nothing,' she said.

'It is with us. I'm always dead regular.'

Their sense of closeness had never taken in anything like this. Pregnancy was horizon stuff, way over yonder in the future. It was something to be talked about endlessly, of course, but it was no part of the here-and-now.

Except suddenly it was. It was a reality right now, in this room – a grim reality, too, if Donna's expression was anything to go by. The untimely occurrence put Nicola at a loss. She didn't know how she should feel, let alone what she should say.

'You mean it was with Jan . . .'

Donna glared.

'I'm not a blimmin' slag, Nicola. Of course it was Jan. He's the only one I've ever loved.'

Nicola felt she was walking on egg shells.

'I didn't know you'd . . .'

'No, well,' Donna spluttered, 'I wasn't going to take an ad out on PJ's Radio Rocket, was I?'

'I'm your best friend,' Nicola pointed out. 'We always said we'd tell each other when we . . .'

'That was when we were kids.'

Nicola sniffed.

'What was it like?'

'Nothing special.'

'Donna!'

'Well, it wasn't.' Donna was less spiky now. 'I mean, he was a great kisser, that part was all right. But the rest . . .' She made a face. 'All I could think about really was I hope nobody sees us.'

'Why? Where the heck were you?'

'That day we went to Cragside. The day we got engaged.' Nicola's face hardened. 'Or muggins here thought we did.'

'Just that once?' Nicola ventured.

'Just that once,' Donna sighed. 'Seems it was enough.'

Nicola thought she should come up with a few practical suggestions.

'Why don't you talk to Lisa?' she said. 'She'd know what to do.'

'Forget that,' Donna said, making the face again. 'First thing she'd do would be to tell me dad, wouldn't it?'

Something more practical than that, then, Nicola thought. It seemed odd, being thrust beyond childhood like this, after pretending so long that it was already miles behind them. Nicola wasn't sure she liked it, the chilly sense of reality, the prospect of Donna having to be responsible — *having to pay* — for her actions.

'Have you done a test or anything?'

'What's the point?'

'So that you'll know for certain, that's the point.'

'I don't want to know for certain, do I?' Donna said.

'But you can't . . .'

Head-in-the-sand was crazy, Nicola thought. But it was typical, too. Left to her own devices, Donna would go on half-kidding to herself she wasn't pregnant until the day the baby popped out.

'Look, I'll help you. We'll go to the chemist and . . .'

'No.'

'But why not?'

Nicola had a vision of the future: Donna with a pram, her hair in curlers, face drained of animation and hope, shuffling down the road in carpet slippers while her jammy-faced baby screamed and screamed . . .

'Because,' Donna said, 'I'm probably wrong and everything will be OK again in a few days.' She looked Nicola straight in the face. 'Promise you won't say anything?'

41

'But . . . ' Nicola sighed, powerless before her mate's entreaty. 'OK, I promise.'

'Great.' The change in Donna was immediate. 'Now let's forget all that boring stuff and go see what there is to eat. I'm starving.'

* * *

Just after four on Thursday afternoon Charlie went to Steve Rettega's recording studio. She had agreed, reluctantly, to let PJ come with her.

She couldn't swear to it, but she was pretty sure she was going through a weird season with boys. Maybe it happened to every girl at least once in her teenage life. Yesterday, coming out of her house, she had been practically tramped into the road by Gill, mooching home from his work. He had walked right into her. After a half-hearted apology he asked her a couple of things about her record, then, right out of the blue, he actually tried to date her.

That had been strange enough, but now, to top it, she had the self-styled King of Cool dangling alongside, bouncing from foot to foot like he was plugged into a power unit.

'I don't know why you have to tag along,' she said.

'I want an intro to the man, that's all.'

Charlie explained she was only seeing Steve to ask if there was any news about the date her record would be released.

'Easy peasy,' PJ said. 'You say, "Hey man, what date's my debut, and this here's my friend PJ, the number one Junior DJ."'

'You're priceless,' Charlie said, ringing the bell on the studio door.

'I know. Spread the word.'

The door was opened by Jazz. He smiled.

42

'Hiya, Charlie. How goes it, man?'

'Great, thank you.' PJ nudged her. 'Jazz, this is my friend PJ.'

'Yeah, we already met. He was looking for Steve.'

Charlie asked if Steve was there. She had been ringing his home number, but there was no reply.

'He's away,' Jazz said.

'Away? Where?'

Jazz pointed out that he wasn't Steve's private personal secretary. He repeated what he had already told PJ, that Rettega simply hired the studio facilities when he wanted to cut a disc.

Charlie insisted that somebody must know where he was and when he would be back. Her record, she said, was due out any time.

Jazz looked thoughtful for a bit, then he went back inside, telling Charlie to hang on.

'Didn't he say anything to you about going away?' PJ said.

'No. But he does have other people to look after, I'm not his only client.'

Jazz came back.

'U. S. of A.,' he said.

Charlie blinked at him, not quite understanding.

'That's where he is,' Jazz told her. 'Gone stateside, man.'

'America?' PJ said, impressed.

'That's all the info I could get. Oh, plus it's got something to do with your number.' Jazz winked at Charlie. 'Stick with it, kid, stay lucky.'

Jazz went back inside, closing the door. Charlie turned to PJ with a look of purest joy.

'No wonder he didn't tell me!' she squealed.

'You what?'

'He wants to bring out my record in America as well! Only he didn't want me to know till he'd got it all fixed up! Oh, PJ, I really am going to be a star!'

* * *

Gill was working on the gearbox of an elderly saloon when the boss, Mr Fletcher, drove a smooth-looking coupé into the garage. He parked it near the door and came across.

'It's in for a few bits and pieces,' he told Gill, pointing to the car, 'but you can start by tuning the engine, right?'

Gill said he could fit it in tomorrow.

'Good. So how's it going, lad?'

'Fine, thanks.'

'Ronnie says you're shaping well.'

Gill looked surprised.

'He said that?'

'He did. Listen, son, I know he's a bit of an old vinegar face, but he knows his job, does Ronnie. Knows cars inside out. You could learn a lot from him.'

If you say so, Gill thought.

'Now,' Fletcher said, 'the thing is this – I've got to go early today, my wife's got some people coming. Ronnie's off too. Do you reckon I could trust you to lock up?'

'Well, yeah.' Gill smiled, flattered to be given the responsibility. 'Yeah, of course, no problem.'

He worked steadily until knocking-off time. When he had closed up the gearbox, put away his tools and washed his hands, he wandered round the garage, savouring the quiet, relishing the fact that he had the place to himself. He took the keys from the office and went round locking the side exits and the gates at the rear service bay. Back in the main garage he stood for a minute, mentally checking that he had secured all the minor doors and switched off all the lights, apart from the ones in here.

On his way to lock the main doors he stopped to admire the car Fletcher had brought in. It was a classy little model, built for comfort and speed. He sauntered

44

across and took a closer look. If he ever had the money, this would be one of the three cars he would own.

He opened the door and got in, smelling rich leather, feeling its resilience as he sank into the driver's seat. He put his hands on the wheel and had a sudden and vivid memory of speed. It had been exciting, joy-riding in that other car. Maybe too exciting: he believed he had lost control of himself and the car, a few times. Even so, he had never known a thrill like it . . .

He stroked the smooth steering wheel, dropped one hand to the ignition and turned the key. The engine purred to life. Not much tuning needed there, he thought. He revved it gently, making it growl. An idea began to form.

* * *

Some fine amateur acting was going on at the Dobson house as Mary O'Malley prepared to leave for the Grove. When she asked if any of the girls were coming along with her, excuses were made with studied casualness. Nicola said that perhaps she would be along later, but first she had an essay to write. Debbie and Jemma said they would be along later, too, but like Nicola they found themselves busy right now.

As soon as the front door closed, Kath shot into action.

'Come on, hurry up, we've all got to get changed yet. They'll be here in an hour . . .'

As the girls were marshalled towards their rooms Debbie whispered to Jemma that Nicola had been allowed to ask Donna to the party.

'It's not fair,' Jemma whispered. 'If she can have her friends why can't I have mine?'

Kath heard that.

'Would your friends want to come?' she asked Jemma.

45

'No. But it's still not fair.'

Kath asked Nicola if Donna had decided to come.

'I hope so.' Since Donna had dropped her bombshell, Nicola wasn't sure of very much. 'I don't know,' she added vaguely.

Meanwhile, in the kitchen at Byker Grove, Brad, Fraser, Duncan and PJ were getting the food ready for *their* surprise party. Brad was unpacking a carton of soft drinks, Fraser and PJ were making sandwiches and Duncan, mindful of the expense, was watching them.

'That's too much margarine,' he cautioned as PJ slapped it on.

Fraser looked up from the bowl he had just half-filled with tinned sardines.

'Duncan,' he said. 'Do us a favour, eh?'

'Yeah – naff off,' PJ said.

Alison breezed in, rubbing her hands.

'Need any help, lads?'

Fraser asked her if you mashed sardines with milk.

'Dash of vinegar,' she said, and turned to Brad. 'Made any progress with Geoff?'

'Over what?'

'Your love affair.'

'Which one?'

'Rosie, of course.'

'Of course.' He shook his head. 'He won't budge.'

Brad detected none of the mockery in Alison now, no tendency to taunt him. Maybe she had thought better of it. Whatever the reason, he was grateful.

'I didn't know you were fond of animals,' she said.

'There's a lot about me you don't know, isn't there?'

Smiling, she said, 'How would you like me to have a go?'

'Ali, you're a gem!'

Brad grabbed her by the shoulders and kissed her.

46

'I'm not doing it for you,' she told him, her cheeks colouring. 'I'm doing it for Rosie.'

Across town Charlie was leaving the house, dressed for the party at the Grove. As she walked along she re-ran her record in her head, hearing her own voice clearly, letting the tune dictate the rhythm of her steps. Tonight she was full of self-confidence. She was on the way up and she *felt* as if she was. She was one of the winners. Quite apart from that, she was aware of the impact created by the combination of her hairdo, make-up and clothes. She was looking good and she knew it. When a car horn toot-tooted somewhere behind her, she assumed it was some young bloke registering his approval.

It sounded again and she turned. The car drew up alongside her. She ducked down and looked in. Gill was at the wheel.

'Want a lift, Blondie?'

She frowned at him.

'Whose car's that?'

'A mate's,' Gill said smoothly. 'He's lent it us for the evening.'

'You're not old enough to drive!'

Gill smirked and did a slow blink.

'When it comes to driving I could teach Nigel Mansell a trick or two.'

'You're off your trolley,' Charlie said.

'So who's going to know?' Gill leaned across and looked her up and down. 'Where you off to, anyway?'

She told him there was a party at the Grove.

'Beats me why you want to waste your time,' he said.

'I like the people who go there.'

'You'd sooner be with that bunch of morons than come for a drive with us?'

'That's right.'

'Listen . . . ' Gill glanced right and left, as if somebody

47

might be eavesdropping. 'We could go out Whitley Bay or somewhere. Plenty of nice little pubs.'

Charlie stood back, exuding disdain.

'You're not old enough to go in a pub,' she said, 'you're not old enough to drive, and in my opinion you're not old enough to be let out on your own.'

'So you're not coming, then?'

'No I'm blimmin' not.'

'It's your loss, superstar.'

Charlie watched the car move off. She wondered if Gill would ever realise what a prawn he made of himself, especially when he tried to come on like a big man.

By the time she got to the Grove quite a lot of the kids were gathered in the main room for the party. Brad and Alison were there, too. PJ was bringing in plates of sandwiches from the kitchen and Fraser was attending to the layout. Mrs O'Malley watched him, blissfully unaware of what was really going on.

As PJ came past Alison he told her he had a surprise for her. She asked what it was, but he said it wouldn't be a surprise if he told her. He moved on, getting to Fraser just as Mrs O'Malley was telling him what a good brother he was, and how tickled pink his sister would be with this lovely surprise.

'Right,' PJ said, cutting in. 'Let's get this show on the road, partner.'

Fraser stared blankly at him.

'The announcement,' PJ hissed. 'Make the announcement, man.'

At that moment Debbie and Jemma came in and crossed to where Mrs O'Malley was standing.

'Gran,' Debbie said, 'Mam says please could you come home for a few minutes.'

'What for?'

'She's making this cake and it's gone all wrong,' Jemma said.

'I can't come just now, lovie. I want to be here to see Spuggie's face when she walks in.'

Fraser had gone shy about making the announcement. PJ decided he would do it. He cleared his throat loudly and addressed the assembly.

'OK, folks. You've all been wanting to know the identity of tonight's mystery guest. So I'm delighted to announce – '

'Come on, Gran!' Jemma called from the door. 'Mum says it's important!'

'Oh, all right,' Mrs O'Malley grouched, crossing the room. 'Just for a minute, though.'

Fraser looked on helplessly as the girls and their gran disappeared through the door.

'Well get on with it, then,' Brad yelled at PJ.

There was a chorus of agreement.

'We're entitled to know who it is,' Duncan muttered. 'They're blimmin' costing us enough.'

At the centre of the growing hubbub Fraser and PJ stared at each other, speechless.

* * *

Winston was cleaning his bike at the front of the house when Gill drew up in the borrowed coupé. Winston stopped what he was doing and approached the car, peering to see through the windshield.

'Fancy a ride, shrimp?'

Winston came closer and looked through the open side window.

'Gill?' he said. Their eyes met and his face lit up. 'Gill!'

'Well, yes or no, man? I've not got all night.'

'Yes!' Winston said.

He abandoned his bike at the front door and jumped into the car. They drove off while he was still fiddling with the seat belt.

'So whose is this, then?'

'Borrowed it,' Gill said.

'From work?'

'What you don't know can't hurt you, right?'

Winston nodded, keeping his eye on the road, enjoying the way the speed was climbing, glad as anything to be back with his mate.

'Won't you get in bother?'

Gill sighed.

'Listen,' he said, 'if you want to bottle out, just say the word.'

'No, no,' Winston said hastily. 'I don't, man.'

'Right, then.' Gill put his foot down a little harder. 'Sit back and enjoy the ride. Gillespie's guided tour.'

* * *

On the linen-covered dining table at the Dobsons' house, a beautifully decorated birthday cake had pride of place at the centre of a lavish spread. Family and friends stood in a group watching the door to the hallway, waiting for Mrs O'Malley to arrive.

'Hush, everybody,' Kath said, even though there had been hardly a sound since they gathered there. 'She'll be here in a minute.' She turned to Nicola. 'I thought you said Donna was coming?'

'I said she might.'

The front door opened. Debbie and Jemma came in on either side of their gran.

'Here she is!' the girls yelled as they steered the old lady into the lounge.

'Surprise, surprise!' everybody shouted.

Mary O'Malley had never been so taken aback in her life. She stood there, hands clasped, looking radiant as any girl while the cheers and good wishes tumbled over her. One by one the grandchildren kissed her cheek, followed by Kath, then Alan, then all the other relatives and friends.

When the commotion died down Mary found herself quite tearful.

'I don't know what to say, I really don't.'

'Don't say anything, Gran,' Nicola told her. 'Just enjoy yourself.'

There was a knock at the door and a second later Geoff let himself in. He went straight to the party girl, kissed her and wished her a happy birthday.

'You're just in time to drink a toast,' Alan told him.

'My pleasure,' Geoff said. 'I can't stay too long though, got to get back. It's not often I get invited to two parties on the one night.'

Kath came across the room frowning. She told Alan and Geoff that old Auntie Doris could smell gas.

'Rubbish,' Alan muttered, filling glasses. 'She always was a bit on the neurotic side.'

'No, hang on,' Geoff said, sniffing. 'I think she's right.'

The two men went out to the hall, then to the kitchen. Geoff walked round slowly, taking deep breaths. Alan did the same in the opposite direction. They came back to the hall, sniffed some more, and decided there was a leak in a pipe somewhere between the kitchen door and the foot of the stairs.

'I think,' said Geoff, 'in the interests of safety, everybody should step outside for a while – at least until somebody's been to have a look at it.'

Within five minutes they were all standing in the back garden, shivering. Alan had turned off the gas at the main and called the emergency maintenance service.

'How long do you think they'll be?' Kath said. 'It's getting chilly. We can't keep them out here too long.'

'Hang on,' Geoff said, staring at the fence. 'I've got an idea.' He turned to Alan. 'Any boards loose?'

'Aye.' Alan pointed to a couple hanging at an odd angle. 'I've been meaning to fix them. Why?'

'Makes a handy short cut.'

Geoff pulled the planks aside and disappeared through the hole.

Back at the Grove the kids in the main room had started singing *Why Are We Waiting*. Fraser and PJ still looked helpless.

'What are we going to do, man?' PJ moaned.

'I don't know. You're usually the one with all the answers.'

'I just hope,' Duncan said darkly, 'you're not wasting our petty cash under false pretences, that's all.'

Fraser and PJ, in unison, told Duncan to shut up.

The noise in the room died down as Geoff appeared. He went straight to Fraser and PJ.

'Lads, I know you've got a bit of a do going on here, but could I ask you a huge favour? I know you both think a lot of Mrs O'Malley . . .'

A few minutes later Geoff led Mary O'Malley, the Dobsons – except Alan, who had to wait for the gas men – and their guests through the gap in the garden fence. They filed across the short cut to the Grove, each carrying part of the birthday-party bounty.

* * *

Gill believed he was really getting the feel of the car. He motored through the streets at speed, moving by gradual stages to the outskirts where there was less traffic. Beside him Winston sat wide-eyed, arms folded, enjoying the trip.

'So what did you ask Charlie out for, anyroad, Gill?'

'Fancied her,' Gill said, his eyes fixed on the road.

'You never. You just wanted to get back at Julie.'

'OK, kid.' Gill adjusted his grip on the wheel. 'You

sussed me. They're all the same, anyroad. I've been a mug. They're none of them worth getting in a sweat over.'

Winston was nodding like an ornamental dog.

'What have I been telling you, man?' he said.

'As they approached a wider stretch of road Gill put his foot down still further.

'Right,' he said grimly. 'Let's see what this baby can really do.'

The car surged forward. Winston glanced sideways.

'Watch it, Gill,' he murmured.

'Stay cool, man.'

Winston's eyes widened as the car got faster still. He could hear the wind whizz and rumble over the roof and along the sides. He didn't dare look at the speedo. He gripped the sides of the seat, hoping Gill didn't hear him when he gulped.

* * *

The party at the Grove was going with a bang. There was an abundance of food and plenty of soft drinks, the kids and the OAPs mingled freely and they even boogied together to PJ's funky music. At the height of the thrash Mary O'Malley approached Fraser and told him how surprised she was that Spuggie hadn't shown up yet.

'She's not coming,' Fraser told her. 'She doesn't want to go anywhere much, lately.'

The information appeared to sadden Mary.

'After all that trouble you've gone to for her, as well,' she said.

Fraser grinned.

'The party wasn't for her. It was for you.'

'For *me*?'

'You've been well good to us. But we didn't know they were going to make you a proper party at home.'

'But this is a proper party,' Mary beamed. 'It's the best blimmin' party I've ever had.'

As she gave Fraser a big kiss, Alison sidled up to Geoff.

'It's very rewarding to make an old person happy, isn't it?' she said.

Geoff narrowed his eyes at her.

'Do I get the feeling I'm being set up?'

'I was only thinking, wouldn't it be even more rewarding to make an old horse happy?'

'No.'

Alison frowned.

'No?'

'No. It's not on, girl. I've enough to worry about with this menagerie here without adding any four-legged ones.' Geoff turned suddenly on Brad, who had wandered across from the doorway. 'In future, don't get women to do your dirty work, sunshine!'

Donna chose that moment to make her entrance, dressed to kill. She flounced around the room for a while, advertising her presence, and finally located Nicola.

'Your dad told me you were here. He said to tell you that the gas people are fixing the leak. He'll be over soon.'

'Good.' Nicola smiled, but her eyes stayed serious. 'I'm glad you came.'

'Why wouldn't I? I love a good party. And this one looks a heap better than I expected.'

'Yeah,' Nicola agreed, 'it's turned out great.' She looked at Donna with a trace of concern. 'Are you OK?'

'Me? I'm fantastic.'

'I mean . . . ' Nicola moved closer and lowered her voice. 'Has something happened . . . you know?'

'Yeah,' Donna said, 'I bought a new top today.' She did a twirl. 'Like it?'

'Donna . . . '

PJ banged loudly on a table, attracting everybody's attention.

'And now, ladies and gentlemen, guys and gals,' he cried, 'we've got a super-special treat for you. The first preview of a sound that's going to be a mega hit, recorded by our very own little Geordie superstar, Charlie Charlton. Madonna eat your heart out!'

He touched a switch on his gear and Charlie's record began. Everyone applauded. Except Donna.

PJ came over and Charlie asked him how he got hold of the record. He explained that he had gone back to the studio and had a word with Jazz. He had a copy of the master tape and was persuaded to part with it when PJ told him it was for a special occasion.

'Hey, you don't mind, do you?'

'No, no,' Charlie said, flushed with pleasure. 'Of course I don't mind. It's wonderful. Thank you, PJ.'

'Think nothing of it.' He went back to the table where the gear was set up and Charlie went with him. He nodded towards the tape deck. 'It's the business that, girl.'

'You really think so?'

'Take it from an expert. You've got a winner there.'

Charlie was suddenly seized with delicious impatience.

'I can't wait for Steve to get back from America!' she said, hugging herself. 'That's when it'll all really start happening.'

Debbie came to the table and stood staring at PJ until he was forced to look at her.

'Will you dance with us?' she said.

'Er, sorry, kid.' PJ made a show of twirling knobs and checking levels. 'Got to stay with the decks, keep the party going.'

Debbie looked around. Brad was standing nearby.

She told PJ he could look after the equipment for a while.

'You're very good at it, aren't you, Brad?'

Brad nodded, coming across.

'I have spun the odd platter in my time, yes.'

'See?' Debbie said, holding out her hand to PJ.

They went on to the dance floor together, PJ throwing Brad a heavy look. Alison appeared at the side of the table.

'He'll not thank you for that,' she told Brad.

'Who wants thanks?' He flipped back the turntable arm and put on a new record. 'This gives me a chance to play what I want.' A very smoochy number began to flow from the speakers. 'Remember this?' he said.

Alison came towards him.

'You played it at Donna's party,' she said, getting close enough for him to catch her perfume. 'We were dancing when Mike walked in.'

'Forget Mike, hmm? Just for five minutes?'

Across the room Donna suddenly stopped talking when she heard the music. She stood listening for a couple of seconds.

'Oh, no!'

Nicola frowned, worried suddenly.

'What?'

'They played that at my party,' Donna said. 'The night I met Jan.'

* * *

Winston was frightened now. As they had ploughed round the last corner, tyres squealing, he had looked at the speedometer. It was showing seventy-five. On a bend! Several times he'd asked Gill to slow down but he didn't respond. His hands were locked on the steering wheel and he stared through the windshield without blinking. He looked supremely confident, but Winston didn't believe he was really in control of the car. The sound of the engine rose and fell too much, they swayed too often on straight stretches of road. Twice, going into bends, Winston had been sure they were going to turn over.

They were bombing along a straight stretch now, the engine roaring as once again Gill pushed his foot to the floor. Up ahead Winston saw a zebra-crossing. Two people appeared to be dithering, not sure if they should step out.

'You're going too fast!' Winston howled, hearing the fear in his voice. 'There's somebody crossing!'

Gill drove on, lowering his head a fraction as they closed on the zebra. The people had come several feet from the pavement and were trying to jump back. The car swerved but the speed didn't slacken.

'Stop, man!' Winston screamed. 'You knocked 'em over!'

'I never,' Gill grunted, glancing in the mirror.

'So why'd you swerve, then?'

'Because you blimmin' screeched down me lughole.' Gill took a swift look in the mirror again. 'The bloke's walking away.'

'There were two of them . . . '

'Rubbish. You want to get your eyes tested.'

Winston began to turn white. Gill kept driving, pushing the engine to its limit. Panic suddenly gripped Winston. He tugged at the door handle.

'I tell you, you hit someone, man! I want out!'

'I didn't hit anybody.'

'You did, man! You're a piggin' lunatic! Let me out!'

Gill slammed his foot on the brake and the car skidded to a halt.

'OK,' he said, not looking at Winston. 'If that's the way you feel.'

Winston opened the door and climbed out shakily.

'Gill, man . . . ' He stood at the side of the road, bent over to look through the open door. 'Listen . . . '

'See you, loser,' Gill said.

He shut the door, threw the engine in gear and tore away from the roadside.

Ten minutes later he arrived back at Fletcher's Garage. He drove into the yard, killed the engine and got out. He hunted around and found a torch, telling himself he was only doing this to prove what he had already told Winston – he hadn't hit anybody.

He walked along the near side of the car, playing the torch beam on the paintwork. Not a mark. He sucked his teeth absently, shining the light further back. He froze suddenly, staring. He crouched, adjusting the angle of the torch beam. There was damaged paintwork at the rear, on the downward curve of the wing. He fingered it for a moment, then stood up sharply, feeling panic gather in his throat. He didn't know what he should do. In the silence of the yard he heard his trembling breath, felt the sweat cold on the back of his neck.

God, oh God, he thought. *What am I going to do?*

CHAPTER THREE

As time passed the panic subsided. Gill was able to think without his mind throwing up disaster pictures – being hauled away by the police, landing in jail, then the horror-show life of a young convict. He stood in the half-dark garage, thinking hard, staring at the scratched paintwork on the car. The damage was there, it existed and had to be faced. If he wasn't to suffer damage himself as a result, he would have to undo the harm he'd done the car. That was the first part. The second part – what to do about maybe having hit someone – would have to wait. One thing at a time, that was the only formula that got a person anywhere.

He hunted around the garage and found the mobile spraying equipment. He had never used it, but he had watched other people and he had a rough idea how to go about doing a cover-up. He wheeled the gear across the workshop and stood back, surveying the job.

First he'd need to treat the paintwork, buffing out the scratches so the surface was smooth. Then he would have to prime the metal and find paint of a matching colour. If there wasn't any in stock he would have to mix other colours until he got the shade he needed. Then would come the spraying. It would have to be done with great care, so the margin between new and old paint didn't show. It was a job calling for skill and patience. And plenty of time. He looked at the clock. It was twenty past eleven. He had time, anyway. He would have to pick up the skill and patience as he went along.

The early stages went slowly. Gill wasn't used to this kind of work, by instinct and experience he was a mechanic. As the minutes passed he developed a lot of respect for paint sprayers. The preparation alone was a killer; when it came to setting up the spray-gun he began to wonder if he would ever manage it at all. Sweat ran over his hands, making him clumsy. He noticed, too, that he was beginning to shake. Panic began to swell up in him again.

He stopped and reminded himself what would happen if he didn't get this job done before daylight. The boss would demand to know what happened. Gill would fumble for a convincing lie, and as he delivered the only pathetic specimen he could come up with, the trust and friendliness between them would evaporate. Before Gill knew it he would be answering questions put by a policeman who would just happen to be investigating a nasty hit-and-run case . . .

Sheer fright made him take a grip on himself. He crouched by the car, hoisted the gun to shoulder height, steadied it and squeezed the trigger. A smudge of paint landed on the wing. It was the right colour but the shade was wrong. Too dark.

Gill told himself to say calm. It was an easy matter to lighten the shade. All it took was time. He turned and looked at the clock again.

'Blimmin' heck . . .'

He couldn't believe it. It was five past two. It had taken him the best part of three hours to get this far. He would have to work faster, even though he felt he would collapse soon if he didn't have a rest and decent cup of coffee. He knew it was best to press on and rest only when he'd got some progress under his belt. As he unscrewed the paint reservoir from the gun he let out a sigh, wishing with all his heart that he'd just locked up last night and gone home, like any sane individual would have done.

* * *

By seven forty-five the Dobsons were at various stages of

breakfast. As usual there was argument rattling back and forward, this time about the Garden Festival. Debbie had declared she wasn't going.

'If she's not going,' Jemma said, 'I'm not going.'

Alan was trying to be philosophical about all this. The refusals to attend were a change from 'If she can go, *I* can go.' Kath was determined to have the matter settled straight away, with no argument at all.

'We're *all* going,' she said, silencing objections with a wave of her hand. 'If I can put up with this leek contest for the fifth year running, then so can you.'

'Thanks for the support,' Alan murmured.

Jemma pointed out that her dad always won. There was no excitement, no breathless anticipation. It was boring.

Debbie nodded vigorously.

'And I bet she won't go,' she said, pointing to Nicola. 'Last year it was period pains. Bet she'll come up with some dead good reason this year, too.'

'Leave it out, Debbie,' Nicola warned.

'No excuses from anyone this year,' Kath said, firm as ever. 'We're all going, and that's final.'

The mutinous talk went on later, as Debbie and Jemma packed their schoolbags in their bedroom. They still swore they wouldn't go, even though they knew they had no chance of dropping out, not now that Kath had made her final declaration.

'Stupid leek contest,' Jemma muttered, jamming books into her bag. 'If I was grown up I wouldn't have to go.'

'Mum's going,' Debbie pointed out.

'Yeah, but she's a wife. They've got to.'

Debbie finished packing her bag and fastened it.

'Anyway,' she said wistfully, '*I* might be having period pains this year.'

Jemma glared at her.

'You haven't even started,' she said.

'That's what *you* think.'

Jemma was suddenly fascinated.

'Have you?' she said, wide-eyed. 'Have you really? Does it hurt a lot?'

Debbie flounced out on to the landing.

'You've got to suffer when you're a woman,' she said over her shoulder.

Jemma came out of the bedroom after her.

'You're blimmin' twelve years old!'

Debbie strode on down the stairs.

'Old enough to wear a bra,' she said airily. 'Which is more than I can say for some.'

As the girls were leaving for school, over at the Byker Arms Jim Bell was coming downstairs into the bar, singing cheerily.

'Here comes the bride,' he warbled, 'all dressed in white . . .'

At the bottom of the stairs he turned and shouted back to Lisa, who was on the landing.

'Only in your case, a little black leather number might be more in keeping.'

'Blimmin' cheek!' she yelled.

A fluffy slipper came hurtling down the stairwell, just missing Jim's head. He turned into the bar, laughing, and was surprised to find Donna there, packing her schoolbag.

'Were you wondering why I was singing that this early on a Friday morning, pet?'

Donna hadn't been listening.

'What?' she said.

Jim moved close, turning on his adoring-daddy routine.

'Donna, lovie – you know Lisa and me have been thinking of getting hitched for a while now?'

Donna looked up from her bag. She was wearing her unshockable face.

62

'Well you're doing it today,' she said.

Jim looked surprised.

'How did you know?'

'Heard you both blabbing on about it in the bath-room, didn't I?'

'So it's OK with you?'

'Of course,' Donna said without enthusiasm. 'Why wouldn't it be? Congratulations.'

'Sorry you won't have time to buy a new outfit, pet.'

Donna narrowed her eyes at him.

'You want us there?' she said.

He told her he wouldn't go without her, and looked as though he meant it. All right then, she said, she would come to the wedding.

'Smashing,' Jim said. 'So I'll pick you up from school. You'll just have time to dash back here, change into a frock, then off to the registry office.'

'Dad, I haven't even washed me hair. It's a right mess.'

Jim smiled at her, all dew-eyed, and told her she would still look a little stunner, if he knew his Donna.

* * *

By five past eight Winston had been leaning on the wall outside Gill's house for more than ten minutes. When he saw Carl come down the path he began to whistle, trying to look cool. Carl came straight up and put his face a couple of inches from Winston's.

'Maybe if I shoved me fist in your gob, you'd be more in tune.'

Winston stopped whistling.

'I'd keep your fist well away from my gob,' he said. 'My dad's bigger than you. Much bigger.'

Carl took that in. He moved back, but he kept the hard look.

'You want to stop hanging around here, too,' he warned. 'You're giving me eye-ache.'

Winston felt a bit bolder now. He said he was waiting for his mate, and there was no law against that.

'Depends whose laws you go by, doesn't it?'

Carl sauntered away, whistling the same tune as Winston, only louder and a lot more out of tune. Winston watched him go, wishing he was big enough to lay a bit of terror on the likes of Carl.

'What do you want, shrimp?'

Winston jumped as Gill spoke. He hadn't seen him come along the path.

'Did you sleep all right, Gill?'

'What kind of a wally question is that?'

'I didn't,' Winston said. 'Not for a second. I kept on thinking about that accident – over and over and over again.'

'For pete's sake, kid,' Gill yelled, 'there *was* no blimmin' accident!'

Along the road Carl stopped. He turned at the sound of Gill's raised voice.

Winston blinked defiantly.

'What did we brush against, then?' he demanded hotly. 'What fell over in the road? Answer me that!'

Gill had hardly slept. His nerves were a frazzle. He glared at his little mate and felt rage bubble up in his chest.

'I'm not telling you again, Winston! You're imagining it! Nothing happened! Got it?'

He turned and stomped off.

The working day went as well as he could have hoped, which wasn't too well at all, but at least there were no emergencies. In daylight, the paint job on the car looked good. Excellent, in fact. Desperation had made quite a paint sprayer out of him. It was true that if he examined the job really hard he could see the margin between new and old paint, but that was only if he looked *really* hard.

As the morning wore on he glanced at the spray job often. The more he looked the more obvious the new paint appeared. After a while he wondered if it was just as obvious to everyone else. By eleven o'clock it was glaring – the paint had been patched and anybody with half an eye could see that.

Imagination! he told himself fiercely. It had looked all right as soon as he came in, hadn't it? He'd glanced at the car as he crossed the workshop and for a second he thought something magical had happened; he couldn't see the new paint job at all, it was as if it had never been necessary. That was the thing to remember: people glanced at the car casually, they weren't looking for a new paint job, so they wouldn't see one.

He worked hard on the engine, taking only half an hour for his lunch so he could strip down the gearbox and give it a thorough clean. After that he would fit a new oil filter. And then do anything else that was needed.

The fact was, he didn't want to move away from the car. He was scared in case somebody started snooping, looking for something wrong. That was crazy, of course, he knew it was. But he couldn't help himself. He had to stay close to the car.

Late in the afternoon he raised his head from under the bonnet and noticed another apprentice at the rear of the car, running his hand over the area where the new paint had been sprayed. Gill froze. The apprentice glanced up at him.

'Nice motor,' he said.

'You want something?' Gill demanded.

The apprentice came along and put his head under the bonnet.

'I was wondering if you'd be much longer on this.

Only Ronnie wants us to start on the spark plugs, sharpish.'

Gill stuck his face close to the apprentice's and addressed him through clenched teeth.

'Get off my back, will you? I'm not a blimmin' machine. I'll be ready when I'm ready, all right?'

The apprentice backed off, startled.

'Right,' he said, moving away. 'Fine.'

* * *

Geoff was finally getting around to mowing the grass at the front of the Grove. Nearby, as he worked, Alison was painting a climbing frame. After a few lengths of the grass Geoff paused and leaned on the handle of the lawnmower.

'Shocking, isn't it,' he puffed. 'This is the most exercise I get these days. And you're looking at a lad who used to play football for his county.'

Alison put down the brush and paint pot and stepped back to admire her work.

'I like men with footballers' thighs,' she said absently.

'Mike's got a good pair, then? How is the lad?'

'All right,' Alison said curtly.

'He hasn't popped round lately. There was a time he took to picking you up. Very gentlemanly of him, I thought.'

'He's been busy,' Alison muttered hastily. 'You're doing a good job there,' she said, changing the subject.

'It'll keep the wilderness at bay for another couple of weeks, eh?'

Alison came across and put her arm round Geoff's shoulder.

'In fact,' she said, squeezing him, 'you're doing a wonderful job.'

'Am I now?' Geoff said, turning suspicious.

'And it'll be perfect.'

'It will, will it?' he frowned. 'What for?'

'She'll be so happy here,' Alison cooed.

'Who will?' Geoff demanded.

'Rosie, of course.'

Geoff stepped back, propping his knuckles on his hips.

'For the umpteenth time,' he said firmly, 'we're not having that horse. We've got enough on our plates as it is.'

'Please?' Alison wheedled, putting her head on one side.

'N.O. No horse.' Geoff was adamant. 'And no more pleading, either.'

Not far away, in the park opposite the Gallaghers' house, Joanne sat on the grass with her box of letters open in front of her. She was reading one of them when Fraser came up behind her.

'You must know what they say off by heart,' he said, making her jump. 'Sorry,' he added, coming round in front of her. 'I didn't mean to scare you.'

'That's all right. I was daydreaming about someone.'

'Three guesses who.'

Joanne smiled.

'I know I go on about Ge Pao. But it's hard to have a brother you've never seen.'

Fraser asked if she'd had another letter yet. She said no, she hadn't, and it would be a month tomorrow since she had last heard from him.

'He doesn't like writing when he hasn't got any news,' she said.

Fraser looked at her for a moment in his serious way, sizing up her mood. He suggested she come down to the Grove with him. It might help to cheer her up.

'No thanks, Fraser. It's not my kind of place. And don't say, "How d'you know if you've never been?"'

'How d'you know if you've never been?' Fraser said, grinning.

'Speedy's been on at me for months to come. I just don't fancy it.'

Fraser said he was going along in ten minutes, in case she changed her mind. Fifteen minutes later they were walking up the path towards the Grove together. On the way they passed Winston, who was lurking so successfully that neither one of them saw him.

'You're dead persuasive, aren't you?' Joanne said.

Fraser shrugged.

'I wouldn't say that. I'm not so good with my sister.'

'Spuggie's been mizzling off a lot, hasn't she?'

'Yeah.' Fraser shrugged again. 'Sisters. Brothers. Who'd have 'em?'

Joanne giggled. She said he was funny. He told her that was a new one on him. He was used to being called 'wimp' and 'brainy bonce', but never funny. Joanne admitted that when he first came to stay, she had thought he was dead stand-offish.

'But you're not, are you? You really care about people.'

'Haway,' Fraser said, embarrassed. 'Any more of that and I'll be sorry I asked you to come.'

They went into the Grove. Out in the grounds, Winston was still hanging around the trees on the edge of the drive, looking miserable, trying to make up his mind whether to go inside or not. It was the first time he had been near the place since everyone had snubbed him over the matter of the super-fertilised leeks.

Young Kelly spotted him standing halfway behind the shade of a low branch, staring at the front of the big house. She went across.

'Wondering if we're still not speaking to you?' she said.

Winston glared at her. He couldn't care less, he told her.

'Then why are you lurking in the bushes?'

'I'm not blimmin' lurking,' he snapped. 'And even if I was, what's it to you?'

'No need to snap my head off,' Kelly said primly.

'Then don't ask piggin' stupid questions.'

She told him he was being horrible, and demanded to know what was up.

'Typical,' Winston said, tut-tutting. 'Flippin' women, they always want to know everything.'

He turned and walked away smartly down the path, leaving Kelly baffled.

Indoors, in the main room, Fraser and Joanne were already deep in conversation with Alison and Brad. Nearby PJ was gently teasing Charlie, asking her if she would get him freebie tickets when she was on *Top of the Pops*. Charlie, more uncomfortable than amused, told him to leave it out – after all, her record hadn't even been released yet.

'A mere formality,' PJ said. 'As soon as your bloke Retteg What's-his-face comes back from the U.S. of A. you'll be mega.'

'Can we talk about something else?' Charlie pleaded. 'I'm bored with discussing me.'

Immediately, as if on cue, Kelly came across and asked Charlie when the record was coming out. PJ, grinning, said it didn't look like her fans were bored. To top it all Fraser brought Joanne across and introduced Charlie to her:

'This is the Grove superstar I was telling you about.'

'I'm *not* a superstar,' Charlie groaned.

'She soon will be, though,' Fraser told Joanne, then introduced her formally to Charlie and Kelly. 'She lives at the place we're staying,' he said, 'only she's adopted.'

Joanne, amused, asked Fraser if he had to go discussing her private life with everyone. Charlie said she knew just how Joanne felt. They laughed. The ice was broken.

In a corner of the room Alison and Brad, on their own now, were discussing the matter of the soon-to-be-executed horse, Rosie, and Geoff's refusal to let her come to Byker Grove to live. They kept their voices low, since Geoff was nearby, serving behind the counter of the snack bar.

'I've tried, several times,' Alison said.

'But did she succeed, this modern-day temptress?' Brad said dramatically.

'Brad, don't.'

'Did she get him begging to have this horse?'

'Brad, shut up, will you?'

'Did she have him pleading to save Rosie?'

'Brad! There's something I want to tell you.'

He suddenly realised she was serious. He told her she had his full attention. She was about to speak when Geoff called from the snack bar.

'When you've finished discussing the weather,' he cried, 'or whatever it is you two sneak off into corners to chat about, we need another box of salt-and-vinegar, and one of peanuts while you're at it.'

Alison, embarrassed, went off to get the supplies.

'We'll find another corner, Ali,' Brad called after her. 'You can bet on it.'

On the other side of the room Debbie had crept up on PJ, Charlie, Kelly, Fraser and Joanne. She got their attention and explained that she wanted them to go to the Garden Festival with her. She promised, with girlish intensity, that it would be a good laugh.

'How does standing around looking at a bunch of manky old leeks get to be a good laugh?' PJ wanted to know.

Fraser said he had absolutely loads of homework to do. Kelly said the Festival sounded dead boring.

'Nah, it isn't,' Debbie insisted. 'You've got all these leeks and all these rosettes and all these people and . . .'

70

She stopped, realising she couldn't make the event sound the least bit interesting. She looked from face to face, her own expression getting more miserable every second.

'So no one's coming, then,' she sighed.

Charlie took pity on her.

'All right,' she said. 'I'll come.'

PJ brightened instantly.

'Yeah, well,' he said, 'nothing's going down round here. So let's hit those leeks.'

Debbie's face lit up. As they were moving away Geoff came across and asked if any of them had seen Duncan. Fraser said he didn't think Duncan had been in tonight. As the gang left Alison came over to Geoff. She asked him if he was worried Duncan was up to his old tricks.

'I wish I could honestly say I wasn't,' Geoff sighed.

'Duncan had a shock when he was found out,' Alison reminded him. 'He's not going to be so stupid again.'

'Nice thinking, pet.' Geoff looked at Alison glumly. 'It's obvious, though, you've never been addicted to anything . . . '

* * *

A few drinks before going to the registry office had made sure the marriage party arrived there in a festive mood. By the time they got back to the Byker Arms they were already into the wedding celebrations. Along with Jim and Lisa were their witnesses – Lisa's pal Rachel and Jim's best friend, Mike. The only one in the party who didn't behave as if it was New Year's Eve was Donna. As they all piled out of the car in the pub car park, she moved a little way apart, watching the others.

Mike started shouting for champagne as soon as he was out in the air. When he realised nobody was going to bring it, he went into the pub himself to fetch a bottle.

Jim in the meantime tried to pick Lisa up in his arms, saying it was time for the bit where he carried her over the threshold. Lisa, swaying, told him he was crazy. He finally got her hoisted in a flurry of arms and legs. Rachel fished her camera out of her hand-bag and took a picture of the pair. By that time Jim was wilting under Lisa's weight. He put her down again. They stood there in the car park, leaning against each other, kissing as Rachel took more photographs.

Mike came rushing out with a bottle of champagne in an ice bucket. He put it on the car bonnet.

'Mr and Mrs Bell,' he announced, 'champagne is served.'

With a struggle he opened the bottle and caused an uproar as the cork shot out and champagne spurted everywhere. Rachel took more pictures. As Mike handed out the glasses Jim beckoned to Donna.

'Come on, lovie. Come and get your pretty face on camera.'

'No, ta,' she said stiffly.

Mike was already proposing a toast.

'So here's to the pair of you – and to the patter of tiny Bell feet, before long.'

Lisa, her face contorted with mock horror, screech-ily informed Mike that they didn't *have* to get married. Donna watched and listened, feeling ice in her heart. Mike was saying they would have real bonny babes if Lisa had anything to do with it. Jim, laughing uproar-iously, swore they had no plans for any offspring. 'Not just yet . . . '

Rachel stuck an arm round Donna's shoulder and breathed boozy fumes in her face.

'You and me'll take it in turns to babysit, won't we, Donna?'

Donna shrugged Rachel's arms off her shoulder.

'Yeah,' Mike said, weaving his way across, 'what would you prefer, Donna? A baby brother or sister?'

Donna couldn't hold her tongue any longer.

'Will you all stop being so blimmin' stupid?' she shouted. 'It's pathetic!'

She turned and strode into the pub, the others staring after her, woozily, as a small lull descended on the celebrations.

It didn't last long. When Jim and Lisa finally got into the bar, followed by Rachel and Mike, Donna was nowhere in sight. Jim called upstairs but there was no response. He went up and looked; Donna wasn't in her room.

He came back downstairs and reminded the others that this was a celebration. The party began in earnest. Jim got behind the bar and made everybody fresh drinks. Lisa fed the jukebox and punched in the numbers of ten different chart hits. All four began to dance, pausing frequently to take more drink.

The party was in full raucous swing when the door opened and Donna came in, followed by Jan and his girlfriend, Kirsten. She walked up to her father and waited until he noticed her.

'Dad,' she said, 'I told you about Jan and Kirsten being over here. Well, I've brought them round to help you and Lisa celebrate. Is that all right?'

The formal little announcement took most of the wind out of Jim's sails.

'Fine,' he said.

Lisa, who wasn't quite so far from sober as she had been pretending, stepped neatly into the breach.

'Of course it's all right, pet,' she said. She beamed at Jan and Kirsten. 'You're both welcome. Now, is champagne all right, or would you prefer a soft drink?'

Jan said he would like a Coke.

'And congratulations on your marriage,' he said.

73

'Yes, from me too,' Kirsten added.

Jim shuffled over to Donna and explained he didn't mind her inviting these two, he was just surprised she was so chummy with them.

'Why?' Donna asked. 'Jan's old news as far as I'm concerned. I'm happy for them both.'

Jim grinned at her warmly.

'If that's the case,' he said, 'I'm proud of you. No more tantrums, eh? My little Donna's growing up.'

'Dad, don't talk like that. It's yuk.'

Jim stood back, raised his glass and addressed the company.

'A toast. To marriage and friendship. Long may they both last.'

They all drank to that.

* * *

In a café near the town centre, Geoff and Duncan were having a coffee and a doughnut together.

'I'm glad you called me,' Geoff said.

'I wasn't sure you meant it when you told me I could.'

Geoff pointed out that he never said what he didn't mean. He assured Duncan he had done the right thing.

'I thought I'd be OK,' Duncan said. 'I just went to watch the other kids playing the machines.'

'But when you were with 'em, you wanted to have a go yourself.'

'It was driving me crazy,' Duncan admitted. 'I couldn't stay and I couldn't leave. I was dying to have a go, only I didn't have any money.'

'And you weren't going to steal again?' Geoff said, narrowing his eyes.

No way, Duncan assured him. He told Geoff that before the trouble with the machines, he had always been dead honest. Geoff said he was still honest, he'd

74

got caught up in something he couldn't handle, that was all.

Even with loads of money in his hands, Duncan went on, he had never, ever stolen any. When his mother had asked him to get money for her with her cashcard, he had never dreamt of taking any for himself.

Geoff said he would let Duncan into a secret.

'I know what it's like to feel out of control,' he said.

Duncan looked shocked.

'You've had the same problem, have you?'

'Not machines in my case. The evil weed.'

Duncan didn't understand.

'Cigarettes,' Geoff said. 'I was a forty-a-day man, once.'

'But you never smoke.'

'Not now, I don't. It wasn't easy giving up, though. I needed my mates around me, especially the ones I could call day and night when I was dying for a puff.'

'So you're doing the same for me, now?' Duncan said.

Geoff winked.

'Happy to oblige, lad.'

Later, as they got into the van, Geoff said he would tell Duncan what helped him out when he was giving up smoking. He got himself an interest, he said. A hobby. It was painting tin soldiers.

'You never!' Duncan said, incredulous.

'Swear I did. And you could do with something to keep you off the streets, too.'

'I'm not painting blimmin' tin soldiers,' Duncan said.

Geoff asked him what he liked. Animals, he said. But his mum had sold their cat because she kept weeing on the carpet. Then they had a hamster, but they found it dead in its wheel one morning. There was a dog after that but it kept biting the neighbours.

'What I really always wanted though,' Duncan said, 'was a donkey.'

Geoff sniffed. It wasn't the most practical idea he had ever heard.

'Not much grazing ground in a tower block, lad.'

Duncan nodded.

'My mum wouldn't let me have one, anyway. She's sick of pets.'

Geoff was staring ahead, his eyes far-away, thoughtful.

'A donkey, eh?' he murmured, turning the key and starting the engine.

* * *

When the Dobson entourage got to the turnstile at the Garden Festival Alan told the cashier they were five kids and two adults. The cashier said that would be twenty-seven pounds. Alan fumbled in his wallet, muttering that fun didn't come cheap these days. At that moment Charlie spotted Greg, her ex-boyfriend, standing behind them in the queue with some of the Denton Burn crowd. The last thing she wanted was an encounter with Greg.

'Sorry, Mr Dobson,' she said, moving away. 'I've just remembered something. Got to go.'

PJ stared at her, mystified. She grabbed his hand.

'Come on,' she whispered hoarsely. 'I'll explain later.'

She ran off, still hanging on to PJ's hand.

'What was that all about?' Alan said.

'Aah, it's not fair,' Debbie said.

'I thought that was Jemma's theme tune,' Kath said.

Debbie said that if Charlie wasn't so nice, she'd thump her.

'You will *not* be thumping anyone, our Debbie,' Alan said. He turned back to the cashier. 'Make that two adults and three kids. Seems we've lost two along the way.'

The Festival was well attended. There was something to take the fancy of anybody interested in gardening, and quite a few stalls for people with no interest in the subject at all. The girls trailed round behind their parents, gazing right and left, yawning occasionally and asking, rather too often, how long it would be until the leek judging started.

Nicola had never found a way of making the visits to the Garden Festival sufferable. Boredom was boredom, there wasn't much you could do to disguise it and kid yourself you were having a great time. The only way to look at it, she supposed, was to see the visit as a penance, a kind of advance payment for something nice that would happen in the future. She was reminding herself of that as they passed a stand with a poster on the front advertising something called The Greenhouse Group. A handsome young man – Nicola guessed his age at around eighteen or nineteen – in a Greenhouse Group T-shirt, was manning the stand. He smiled amiably at the people going past.

'There you go, sir,' he said, offering Alan a leaflet.

Alan brushed it aside and moved on. Nicola wanted to complain to him about his rudeness; simultaneously she wanted to explain to the young man that her dad wasn't usually such a bad-mannered oaf. She did neither, but as they moved along she looked back, wishing the chap would glance her way so she could smile at him.

They eventually joined the gathering in the leek contest hall. While the others watched the judges moving along the rows of leeks, Debbie went for a walk around the hall. She read the various posters, and when she came back she muttered something about giant vegetables, just as the place went quiet.

Kath told her to shush, the judges were about to announce the prize winners.

'I was only saying giant vegetables,' Debbie hissed.

'You heard what your mother said,' Alan snapped, craning forward to hear who had won what.

Third prize went to the Denton Burn Youth Club. There was a loud cheer from their supporters and Greg went forward to accept the trophy on behalf of the club. Nicola nudged Debbie.

'That's why Charlie flew off in a fright,' she whispered.

The second prize was awarded to a Mr and Mrs Tattersall. Blushing with pride they stepped forward to energetic applause and were handed their cup.

'Here we go, then,' Kath murmured as the clapping died down.

The atmosphere grew tense. Contestants eyed each other sideways as the judge consulted his piece of paper, prior to announcing the winner of the first prize. Debbie chose that moment to push forward and address her parents.

'It says there's a giant vegetable competition over there,' she said, pointing to the poster.

'We haven't got any giant vegetables,' Kath said. 'We've got leeks.'

'Yes we have,' Debbie said. 'The Grove has.'

Alan told her to be quiet. The judge cleared his throat and stepped forward.

'First prize, once again, ladies and gentlemen,' he said, 'goes to Mr Alan Dobson for yet another magnificent entry.'

A wave of cheering and clapping rose from Alan's supporters. Kath hugged him as he went forward to collect the trophy.

'Well done, Dad,' Nicola said when he came back. 'We're proud of you.'

'Yeah, we're really proud,' Jemma told him, then added, 'Can I have a pound for the train ride?'

Later, when they were leaving the Festival, Alan

proudly clutching his cup, Debbie resumed an argument that had fizzled on and off ever since she had seen the poster advertising the giant vegetable competition. She demanded to know why she couldn't enter the Grove's leeks. Alan said the competition was a joke, he wouldn't give it the time of day. And he didn't want to hear any more about it.

'No one ever takes any notice of my ideas,' Debbie moaned.

As they passed The Greenhouse Group's stand again Nicola said she wanted to get something – she would catch them up in a minute. She went to the stand, smiling broadly to the lad she had seen earlier.

'Hi. We came past before. I was with my family.'

'Yeah.' The young man grinned. 'I remember.'

'Sorry my dad was so rude to you, only his leeks were being judged.'

'That's all right. When you've got important matters to attend to . . . '

'Anyway, I'd like one of your leaflets, please.'

He handed one over and as he did, she noticed his name badge said PAUL. He asked if she would like to know more about what the group did. She said she would. But another time.

'Me dad'll kill me if I keep them waiting. T'ra.'

As she moved away Paul called after her.

'Did he win?' he yelled.

'Yes,' Nicola shouted back. 'Again!'

* * *

In the short time she had been at the Grove, Joanne seemed to have taken to the place. During a lull in her conversation with Kelly, Fraser asked her if she was glad she had come. Joanne considered the question and finally said that coming here was definitely better than sitting at home thinking about Ge Pao. That prompted another question from Fraser: why did she care so much about this brother if she had never seen him?

'Because he's the only living relation I've got,' Joanne said. 'Because he's stuck in some grotty camp in Hong Kong, while I'm having a great time here. Because he cares about *me*. Does that answer your question?'

'This camp he's in,' Kelly said, 'is it the same as when we go camping, with tents and ropes and stuff?'

Joanne laughed. No, she said, it was a different kind of camp. It had proper buildings, but they were pretty awful.

'I hope and pray Ge Pao can get out of there and be with me.'

'Why doesn't he just leave?'

'I wish it was that simple. He's trying to get permission from the government, but it takes ages. First he's got to prove he's my brother, and that means interviews and questions and forms . . . '

Across the room PJ had put on the demo tape of Charlie's record and was dancing to it with a couple of the kids.

'It's lucky *you* haven't got any brothers or sisters to worry about, eh?' Fraser said to Kelly.

'Yeah,' she said, very quietly, 'lucky . . . '

At that point Charlie marched into the room. She went straight to the ghetto blaster, switched it off and snatched out the tape.

'Hey,' PJ complained. 'What's that for? I thought I'd make you feel better after seeing that ex of yours.'

'I'm sick of hearing it already,' Charlie said. 'And it's *my* record. *I'm* keeping it.'

'Hey, stay cool,' PJ said, looking hurt. 'Do what you like with it. I was only trying to help.'

Meanwhile Alison was in the office, looking through the filing cabinets. Brad came in, closed the door, put a chair against it and sat down.

'Right,' he said. 'No interruptions now until you've told me what's on your mind.'

Alison nodded, took a deep breath, and began.

Outside, two of the kids were sitting on the grass just beyond the office window. They jumped with shock as Brad started whooping and hollering inside the office. A moment later he came rushing out, did a quick jig, let rip with another yell and ran inside again.

Back in the main room Charlie had approached PJ and asked if she could have a word. He said sure, if she wanted to, and asked Joanne and Kelly to excuse him. He and Charlie went to a corner together.

'I'm sorry about blowing my top earlier,' Charlie said.

PJ told her it was all right. Women were allowed to be temperamental. Charlie insisted that it hadn't been fair – the trouble, she believed, was that she was getting funny feelings about this record business. PJ asked her what she meant.

'Well . . . what with Rettega being out of the country for so long, I thought I'd have heard from him by now.'

'He's probably being swept off his feet with the success of your record,' PJ said, doing his best to plug the leak in Charlie's confidence.

She couldn't help having misgivings and doubts, she said. She reminded PJ what happened when he went to the studio looking for Rettega: nothing he had told Charlie seemed to fit the story PJ had been given. PJ tried to wave that aside by saying people in the music business were all like that – creative geniuses and airheads all in one.

'What I'm most bothered about,' Charlie said, 'is my contract.'

PJ frowned.

'What's up with it? Is it no good?'

'I haven't even seen it to find out. Rettega promised me I'd have it two weeks ago.'

'Meanwhile you're rushing down to the post every morning?'

'You got it,' Charlie said, smiling.

'And won't you feel a nana when Rettega comes back, everything's cool, and you're a hit on both sides of the Atlantic.'

The thought seemed to cheer Charlie up.

'I suppose you're right,' she said. 'It's just that we creative geniuses have also got vivid imaginations.'

In that case, PJ told her, she should imagine herself a star.

He turned and saw Donna come in, accompanied by Jan and Kirsten, who had their arms around each other. They went across and joined Fraser, Joanne and Kelly.

'Fraser and Kelly,' Donna said coolly, 'you remember Jan? And this is his girlfriend, Kirsten.'

Jan said it was nice to see them again, and he clearly meant it. Joanne introduced herself and told Jan and Kirsten, just as sincerely, that she was pleased to meet them.

Kelly, blunt as ever, turned to Donna and Jan and asked when they had made friends again.

'Jan and me?' Donna said, sounding surprised. 'We never really fell out, did we?'

Jan didn't seem inclined to argue. He smiled as Charlie and PJ came over.

'If it isn't the Danish dude that all the girls flipped over,' PJ said, grinning.

'Not all of them, PJ,' Donna said. 'This is Jan's girlfriend, Kirsten.'

PJ's grin fell away.

'Sorry. Hope I didn't put my blimmin' foot in it.'

Kirsten smiled and assured PJ it was all right. She and

82

Jan, she said, had been honest with each other about all their relationships. Charlie said she thought that was a dead good idea.

'Great idea,' Donna agreed. 'It saves misunderstandings later.' Turning to Jan she said, 'Come on, let's see who else is around that you know.'

Charlie watched them go.

'Strange threesome,' she said. 'I thought Donna was never going to speak to him ever again.'

'Where Donna and men are concerned,' Kelly said, 'who knows?'

Geoff and Duncan came into the main room as Donna, Jan and Kirsten were approaching another bunch of kids. At that moment Brad and Alison came out of the office, hand in hand, looking highly excited.

'Geoff!' Brad called. 'We missed you!'

He walked straight over to Geoff and, to Geoff's astonishment, planted a smacking great kiss on his cheek. Geoff stared at Alison as he wiped his face.

'Alison, I think we should have a serious chat.'

Alison was trying desperately to look serious and not giggle.

'About a horse,' Geoff added.

* * *

They practically had to throw Gill out of the garage to make him stop working on the car. As the day wore on he had grown more and more convinced that if he left it alone, somehow his secret would be found out. By the time he left the garage, the engine was better tuned than when it was new.

Arriving at the squat where he lived, he was on the way to his room when Carl appeared. A little sneer dangled at the corner of his mouth.

'Hello, Gillespie,' he said.

Gill ignored him and turned the key in the lock.

'I said hello, Gillespie,'

Still ignoring him, Gill opened the door and started to go inside. Carl put out his arm and stopped him. Gill stared at him, staying calm.

'Now is that nice?' Carl drawled. 'Your neighbour is trying to be pally and this is how you treat him.'

'Whatever reason you're being pally for,' Gill said, 'it's bound to be a stitch-up.'

Carl said maybe it was because Gill had no mates and he was feeling sorry for him. Gill told him to get lost.

'First that Julie bird scarpered, then you're slagging it out with your mini mate.'

'Winston?'

'Whatever his name is.' Carl moved closer. 'Take a tip from me, kid. It doesn't do to have your arguments in public. Somebody might hear.'

Gill pushed past and went into his room. He sat down, intending just to rest for a minute before he got cleaned up and had something to eat. But the tension and exhaustion of the day caught up with him in a rush. He fell asleep.

He woke up to a hammering on the door.

'Bog off, Carl,' he yelled.

'It's not Carl,' Winston said. 'It's me.'

'Bog off, Winston.'

'You've got to let me in! It's about the accident!'

Gill shot out of the chair, dived across the room and opened the door.

'Stupid plonker, shouting your head off for everyone to hear.'

He dragged Winston inside and shut the door.

Winston explained, breathlessly. He had seen a hoarding that said something about a hit-and-run accident, so he had tried to get a paper, but they had

84

ll been sold out, so he tried a newspaper vending machine, but it wouldn't work . . .

He stopped, noticing Gill had an evening paper.

He picked it up and looked. Nothing on the front page. He flipped through the sheets. By page five there was still nothing.

'You don't know what you're rabbiting on about, you,' Gill said. 'Anything major and it'd be in here.'

Winston turned to page six and there it was. He swallowed and started to read aloud.

'At approximately nine-thirty yesterday evening, a serious hit-and-run accident occurred on Nethersley Road. Witnesses say a medium-sized saloon car sped off without stopping. There was more than one person in the vehicle . . . ' Winston stopped and looked up from the paper. 'It's us, Gill,' he said. 'It's us.'

They stood looking at one another, Winston openly terrified, Gill pale with shock.

CHAPTER FOUR

After a sleepless night the morning brought Winston no relief, no ray of hope. He sat alone hardly able to eat breakfast, listening to the local radio news. Towards the end there was an update on the hit-and-run. The victim a man, was in Intensive Care at Newcastle Royal Infirmary; a spokesman had described his condition as critical. The police were still appealing for witnesses to the accident.

Winston had never been so scared in his life.

Gill didn't feel any better. After tossing and turning all night, he finally fell into an exhausted sleep around four-thirty. He overslept. When he got to the garage ten minutes late, Ronnie bawled him out and warned him that if he was late again he would feel the punishment where it hurt – in his pay packet.

School work that morning was more baffling than usual for Winston. He couldn't hold an idea for more than a minute and when the teacher asked him to work out simple equations he just stared back, flummoxed. As soon as the lunch bell went he tore out into the yard, got on his bike and pedalled like mad over to the Infirmary.

When he had parked the bike he wandered around the outside of the main building for nearly five minutes bewildered by all the signs. Finally he found one that said RECEPTION/ENQUIRIES. He followed the arrow and went through the big swinging doors. At the desk a kindly-looking woman asked if she could help.

'I've come to enquire . . . ' Winston stopped, realising he didn't even talk that way. 'I want to know how the man who was run over on Thursday is doing.'

The woman asked what the man's name was. Winston wanting to run away, clung grimly to the edge of the desk and forced himself to come up with some kind of answer. He wasn't sure of the name, he said, but the man was knocked down on Nethersley Road, if that was any help.

'His condition's critical,' he added, repeating what he had heard on the radio.

The woman checked the day-book in front of her.

'Sounds like Mr Simmonds,' she said. 'He's in Intensive Care. In a coma.'

Winston stared at her. *Coma*. The word put a chill through him. He swallowed hard a couple of times and tried to wet his tongue.

'Will he die?' he said.

The woman frowned at him. She couldn't say anything about that, she explained, leaning a little closer. She took a good close look at Winston.

'Can I ask who you are?' she said. 'You're obviously not a relative . . .'

'I'm . . . a sort of friend,' Winston gulped.

'Let me take your name, pet, in case Mr Simmonds comes round.'

The woman turned to the table behind her to get her pen. When she turned back Winston had gone.

From the Infirmary he cycled across town to Fletcher's Garage. He managed to attract Gill's attention and they went down the side of the workshop where they wouldn't attract any attention. Winston told Gill what he had learned at the Infirmary.

'He's in a bad way, then,' Gill said.

Winston put it more bluntly: the man was going to die, he was sure of it. Gill scoffed at that, trying to keep up his hard front. He told Winston not to be such a drama queen.

'Lots of people in comas pull through,' he said.

'The woman said "in case he comes round". She doesn't fancy his chances, either.'

'So what can we do about it, eh?' Gill tried not to look

or sound desperate, but that was the way he felt. 'Should we go round the hospital and wait for news? Or maybe you want us to go down the cop shop and give ourselves up, is that it?'

Winston had no idea what to do. That was why he had come to see Gill. To both of them, the situation was like being at the blind end of a cave, with the enemy about to come in through the door any minute. Gill dug his hands in his pockets and leaned against the wall.

'I haven't got any magic answers,' he said. 'We're both in this mess together. Best thing we can do is lie low and hope it blows over.'

'Oh, great.' Winston glared at him. 'It's all right for you, Mr Cool, just getting on with your job as though nothing's happened. But I'm worried piggin' sick.'

Gill rounded on him.

'You think I'm not, eh?'

'Yeah, well, I didn't say – '

'You think I'm sleeping nights? You think I can concentrate on my work? Do you *really* think I'm not worrying about it every second of the blimmin' day? Then think again, mate!'

Winston tried to say something, but Gill turned and stormed back into the garage.

* * *

The day wore on, one long worry with occasional panics as Winston imagined what might happen to him and Gill if they were caught. When school was over he cycled over to the Grove and went in, the first time since the trouble over the leeks.

He wandered around the house aimlessly. It was only four-thirty, so there weren't too many kids there yet. In the games room he found Charlie and PJ playing table

88

tennis against Kelly and Duncan. Winston stood watching them, still distracted, only half his mind on what was happening around him.

'Look what the wind blew in,' PJ said.

Kelly turned and smiled at Winston.

'We *have* forgiven you,' she said, 'in case you didn't know.'

'Blimmin' leeks,' Winston grunted. 'Who cares?'

Kelly observed, out loud, that he was still in a mood. Winston told her to shut up. Duncan told him not to be so horrible. That did it. Winston told them they were all a pain in the neck. He turned to go and almost bumped into Geoff, who had come into the games room with another man.

'There she is,' Geoff beamed, pointing to Charlie. 'Newcastle's answer to Madonna.'

Charlie, embarrassed, pulled a face as they approached her. Geoff introduced the other man as Steve Marlor, a reporter from the *Newcastle Evening Post*.

'You graciously agreed to give an interview a couple of weeks ago,' Geoff said. 'Remember?'

Winston had frozen on the spot when he heard the newcomer was a reporter. He watched as Marlor went off to the club room with Charlie to conduct the interview. As the door closed behind them Winston decided he wouldn't leave just yet.

The interview was an uncomfortable experience for Charlie. Instead of being able to tell her story in a straightforward way, she was asked questions that jumped back and forward in time, and some of them were too personal for her liking. Even when Steve Marlor got down to discussing the main reason for the interview, Charlie felt she was being pushed along in a direction she didn't want to travel.

'The record is due out in the next few weeks,' Steve said, 'is that right?'

'I think so,' Charlie said. 'I mean yes, yes, it is.'

'You don't seem too sure.'

'It's only that my producer is promoting my record in America at the moment and I haven't spoken to him for . . . a few days.'

'So you're going to be a hit on both sides of the Atlantic?'

'I don't know. I mean, I hope so.'

Charlie wondered how all this would look in print. She felt like a child, answering questions on a topic she hadn't studied hard enough, afraid that any second she'd put her foot right in it.

'How do your friends treat you at school?' Steve asked.

'Just the same.'

'There isn't any teasing about your new-found stardom?'

This was all wrong. He might as well have been talking to somebody else.

'Mr Marlor,' Charlie said carefully, 'there isn't any new-found stardom.'

She watched his hard little predator's eyes probing hers, as if he would like to read her thoughts.

'What exactly do you mean, Charlie?'

'My record hasn't come out yet,' she said. 'No one has bought it yet. No one has said they like it yet, except a few of my friends. All I've done is recorded a single. That doesn't make me a star.'

She watched his face turn sour, a feature at a time.

'Well, Charlie,' he said, 'I appreciate your modesty. Let's hope it remains intact when you're famous.'

Charlie fought to stay calm for the rest of the interview, smothering an unreasonable desire to throttle Marlor.

Later, as he was leaving, Winston stopped him. He asked, in an anxious whisper, if he could have a word. Steve told him to fire away.

The words, pent up for so long, tumbled out of Winston.

'It's about a hit-and-run accident on Thursday night . . . Nethersley Road . . . I wondered if they'd found out – '

'Stop!' Steve put up a hand. 'Stop, please. Before you go any further, that's not my department. I'm Entertainment. You want Newsdesk.'

Winston looked defeated. Steve took out his notebook and scribbled down a number. He tore out the page and handed it to Winston.

'There you go. Call that number. Ask for Marianne.'

'Thanks, mate.'

'And I hope your friend, or whoever it is, is going to be all right.'

'Me too,' Winston said, with feeling.

A few minutes later Geoff was passing the Grove's own 'phone box. He stopped, hearing Winston inside, talking earnestly into the mouthpiece.

'I wondered if the police had found out who did it yet,' Winston said. There was a pause. 'No, he's not a relation. Look, could you just tell me whether the cops . . . ' He stopped and nodded a few times. 'Thanks,' he said hastily. 'Bye.'

He put down the receiver, turned and walked into Geoff.

'If I didn't know you better, Winston, I'd say you were acting shiftily. And what was all that about the cops?'

'Blimmin' heck!' Winston went stiff with affront. 'Why can't other people keep their noses out of my business?'

He stamped off in a fury, leaving Geoff to wonder what was up this time.

* * *

Debbie, Duncan and Kelly were playing cards in the

main room. PJ and Charlie were sitting together nearby and Brad was deep in conversation with Alison over by the door. They all looked round as Mary O'Malley walked in. She appeared to be very pleased with herself.

'Right,' she said loudly, to no one in particular. 'That's sorted.'

'Great,' Brad said, mystified. 'What's sorted, Mrs O'Malley?'

'Our Debbie.'

Debbie looked at her gran.

'You can get those leeks dug up, lovie. They're entering a contest tomorrow.'

Debbie was delighted. Alison stepped forward, puzzled, and asked if the rest of them could be let in on the plot. Mary explained, not too patiently, that Debbie had had the wonderful idea of entering the Grove's leeks for the giant vegetable competition. The trouble was, the entries should have been in weeks ago.

'So I had a word,' Mary said.

'Mrs O'Malley!' Brad pretended to be horrified. 'You didn't bribe anyone, did you?'

'I certainly did not. I used my feminine powers of persuasion on my old friend Harry Stanton. The judge.'

'You mean you flirted with him?' Brad said.

'You can wipe that smile off your face, young man,' Mary snapped. 'Just because my bones are old, it doesn't mean I've lost the knack.'

Mary cocked her head suddenly, hearing a conversation behind her. Duncan and Kelly were whispering, but not quietly enough. The gist of their comment was that the competition was a dead stupid idea, but it was the kind of thing that probably amused old people.

Mary turned on them, her scolding face ready. Across the room, oblivious to what was going on between Mary and the kids, Charlie was telling PJ what a fraud she had felt with the reporter.

'I couldn't answer any of his questions,' she said. 'I had to keep making things up.'

'So you were behaving like a star, then,' PJ said.

She told him not to be so flippant. This was serious. She was determined to find out the truth about her recording career. She would go to the Riverfront Club tonight and try to find Dexter – she believed he was the only one who might know anything concrete.

'Going on your own?' PJ asked.

Charlie lowered her head, looking at him through her eyelashes.

'I was sort of hoping . . .'

'Name the time,' PJ said without hesitating. 'Name the place. PJ's your man.'

Charlie hugged him. PJ could hardly believe his luck.

* * *

At five-fifteen Gill was working on a car when the foreman, Ronnie, came over and told him the boss wanted to see him as soon as he had finished the job. Gill was momentarily frozen with shock. He recovered enough to ask Ronnie if he knew what it was about. Ronnie shook his head. As he went away again he told Gill to be sharpish. Mr Fletcher was waiting.

Gill was badly scared. He didn't dare imagine what Fletcher was going to confront him with. Working fast, he finished the job he was on and washed his hands. Setting his jaw and getting ready for anything, he went to the boss's office.

Fletcher was sitting behind his desk, hands spread on top, his expression serious and very businesslike. Gill hovered in the doorway, not knowing what to do with himself. His heart was pounding so hard he was sure the boss would hear it.

'Have a seat, Gill.'

He was surprised when his legs worked. He stilted across the room and sat down opposite the desk. The boss looked at him squarely.

'Have you any idea what I'm about to say?'

Gill's tongue felt like it was stuck to the roof of his mouth.

'No,' he managed to say.

Mr Fletcher tilted his head to one side. He asked Gill how he thought he had been doing.

'What – here?' Gill croaked.

Fletcher laughed. That made Gill feel worse, if anything.

'Where else? Unless you've been moonlighting. How do you rate your performance here, Gill?'

Gill relaxed a little as he realised he wasn't about to be nabbed.

'All right,' he said. 'Well, good, really.'

Fletcher nodded.

'That's what Ronnie tells me. He says you have the makings of a first-class mechanic. Although your time-keeping could do with a brush up.'

'Sorry about that, Mr Fletcher.'

'Right, so long as you see to it.' Fletcher folded his hands on the desk. 'So, I wanted to tell you this myself. Your month's trial is over and I'm taking you on permanently. We'll train you and give you a wage increase of ten pounds a week, plus luncheon vouchers. Is that all right with you?'

Gill was stunned. The shift from abject fear to glowing relief – with a nice surprise thrown in – had been so sudden he felt dizzy.

'Is that satisfactory to you?' Fletcher asked again.

'Blimmin' amazing!' Gill said, and checked himself. 'Sorry. Yes, thank you.'

He couldn't think what else to say. Fletcher told him that was all, unless there was anything further he wanted to know. Gill said, no, nothing at all, and said thanks again. As he was leaving Fletcher called to him.

'Keep up this good work and you could really be going places.'

Gill smiled weakly and left, his mind spinning too hard for him to grab a thought and hold on.

* * *

'Mary's right,' Kelly said. 'We've got to win this competition to get our own back on Denton Burn.'

'It was *my* idea,' Debbie reminded her.

They were still in the main room at the Grove. Duncan, PJ and Charlie were there too. Alison was at the snack bar, helping Brad tidy the counter.

'I'd like to see their faces when we come away with the cup,' PJ said.

Charlie said Greg would go potty. In the cool aftermath of her relationship with him, she could remember how much he hated being beaten at anything. Mary came in as Duncan was reminding Charlie that they hadn't won yet. They wouldn't have a chance of winning at all, Mary said, until they got the leeks dug up.

'Found a use for them, have you?' Geoff said, overhearing her as he came in. 'Boiling us up a nice leek and potato soup, maybe?'

Mary told him haughtily that she was doing nothing of the sort. The leeks, for his information, were being entered in the giant vegetable competition. Geoff said that was good, it would make all the more room.

'Room for what?' Alison asked.

'Didn't you know? We're having a horse to stay.'

Alison stared at him.

'Rosie?'

He smiled.

'How many horses do you know?'

Alison ran to Geoff, hugged him tightly and kissed his cheek. He grinned cheerily as she released him.

'That was almost worth the effort and aggro and hassle this horse is going to create,' he said.

Jemma came bouncing up, eyes dancing, cheeks flushed with excitement.

'She's not going to cause any effort or aggro or other stuff, because I'll look after her every day, and I'll come before school and I'll come after school and I'll feed her and I'll take care of her and – '

'Steady on,' Geoff said. 'She's a horse, Jemma, not a sick elderly relative. And Duncan's going to help you take care of her, aren't you, Duncan?'

'Yeah, I'd like that.'

Jemma turned to Brad and asked if they could please, *please*, go and visit Rosie now. Only if nurse Alison could come to look after him, Brad said. Alison asked Geoff if that would be all right. He told her, and the others, to scarper.

'And get those muscles ready for some paddock building when you get back,' he called after them as they filed out.

Ted Boneo, the rag-and-bone man, was overwhelmed when so many kids turned up to see his old horse.

'I don't know what to say,' he told Alison as he watched them queue up to pat Rosie.

Alison told him there was no need to say anything. It would be a pleasure to take Rosie for him. As they stood talking Jemma came across and asked if Rosie was very old. Ted said she wasn't as old as he was, but she was old enough to retire all the same. When Duncan said he wanted to feed Rosie, Ted slipped him a Polo mint and told him that if he gave her that, she would be his friend for life. As Duncan fed the sweet to the grateful animal Jemma said she would like to ride her. At that, several other kids said they would like to ride her, too.

'I don't see why not,' Ted said.

He asked Alison to excuse him and he set about organising the kids. Brad and Alison snatched the opportunity to slip off for a few moments on their own.

'When *I'm* old and knackered,' Brad said, 'will I get all this attention, do you think?'

'Depends if there's anyone crazy enough around at the time,' Alison said.

Brad smiled at her warmly.

'I was hoping it would be you.'

Alison became a little serious. She asked Brad not to go forward too fast and not to expect too much – after all, they had only been together for twenty-four hours.

'And what a difference a day makes,' Brad said. He saw Alison was about to protest again and he said, 'All right, all right, sweetheart, I was only teasing you.'

They stood in silence for a moment, simply enjoying being close.

'I'm moving out on Sunday,' Alison said. 'I'm going to stay with a girlfriend.'

'You could stay with me.'

Alison shook her head. It was too soon, she told him. She needed to know him better before they lived together.

'Who's talking about living together? I was thinking of two weeks, top whack.'

Alison gave him a playful thump which, by a series of gentle wrestling moves, turned into a cuddle.

Jemma appeared and stared at them reproachfully.

'Will you two stop smooching and come and see Rosie? She's got huge teeth but she won't bite you and she likes carrots.'

'Yes, madam,' Brad said. 'We'll be right over. *When* we've finished smooching.'

* * *

Charlie and PJ got to the Riverfront Club just after nine o'clock. Charlie looked very different from the last time she visited the place – she had on jeans, a sweater and an anorak. As they drew nearer the front of the club she began to get anxious. She stopped a short way from the door and turned to PJ.

'I really appreciate you coming . . .'

'But you want to talk to this Dexter bloke on your own, right?' PJ smiled to reassure her. 'I would if I were in your shoes.' He squeezed her arm. 'You'll be fine.'

Charlie walked forward hesitantly, leaving PJ in the shadows. At the door she knocked sharply and stood back, startled by the noise she had made. A burly doorman opened up and stared at her. Charlie told him she had come to see Dexter. The doorman told her she couldn't come in, he would have to find the gentleman for her. Her turned and shouted Dexter's name, adding that there was a pretty young lady to see him. After a moment Dexter appeared.

'What a surprise. Charlie Charlton.'

She kept the preliminaries to a minimum and came right to the point. She told Dexter she was there because there was something she needed to know from him.

'Ask,' he said.

'Do you know where Rettega is, and what he's doing with my record?'

Dexter looked surprised.

'*Your* record?' he said. 'He hasn't told you?'

'Told me what?'

'About Maddie Brown.'

What, Charlie demanded, did an American superstar have to do with her single?

'It ain't your single any more, sugar.'

'*What?*'

'Maddie Brown heard it, Maddie Brown recorded it, Maddie Brown released it – last week, in the States.'

Charlie was shocked.

'Does Rettega know about it?'

Dexter laughed bitterly.

'*Know* about it? He played the track to her in the first place. Sweetheart, this can be a lousy, rotten, stinking business, and it looks like you've just found out the hard way.'

Charlie could hardly take this in. She asked Dexter if he was sure about what he'd told her.

'As sure as I'm standing here.' He shrugged. 'Looks like he landed us both in it, sweetheart. Should have stuck with me, eh?'

Charlie turned away, completely deflated.

'I'm always around if you want to give it another go,' Dexter said, then caught the look on her face. 'Maybe not yet,' he murmured.

Charlie, numb with shock, walked slowly back to where PJ was waiting. She couldn't explain, not at first, so they walked to the park. Charlie lay on the grass and PJ sat down beside her. Slowly, she told him what Dexter had told her. They both went silent again for a while.

'You don't have to keep quiet,' Charlie said after a few minutes. 'It's OK.'

PJ said he had only been quiet because he had no idea what to say. That had to be a first, Charlie said, managing a smile.

PJ wasn't smiling. If he was twice the size, he told Charlie, and if he had bigger muscles, and if Rettega was there, he'd wallop him for what he had done to her. PJ just couldn't believe it had happened.

'Well, he did it,' Charlie said, resignedly. 'I can't believe it either. Everything I've been hoping and dreaming about, suddenly it's all disappeared. I'd got it all planned, right down to buying my mum a new coat with my first cheque.'

PJ said she could still do it, she could find someone else to produce her.

'No way. Never. I'm not ever going to get involved in this disgusting business again.'

'It's a shame,' PJ said wistfully, 'because you really have got talent.'

'That's not what the other kids are going to say. They'll say I was making it up, spinning some blimmin' fantasy. I'm going to look a right nana.'

'They won't be like that,' PJ said. 'And if some of them are, stuff 'em. Who cares?'

'I do,' Charlie said.

* * *

Just after ten on Saturday morning a large gang of kids, under the supervision of Geoff, gathered on a stretch of common land near the Garden Festival site. Carl hovered in the background, trying to look inconspicuous.

'While we're together,' Geoff announced, 'if anyone gets lost we'll meet you back here. Got that?'

'Blimmin' heck, Geoff,' Nicola complained, 'we're not little kids.'

Geoff gave her a warning look.

'You may not be little, Nicola –'

'And I'm not either,' Jemma piped up.

'Back at this spot if you get lost,' Geoff said, giving it the hard edge of authority. 'And I don't care if you're blimmin' seventy. Oops, sorry, Mary.'

Just then Donna made her appearance, arm-in-arm with Jan on one side and Kirsten on the other. Unknown to the others, she had spent a large part of the previous afternoon and evening shopping with Kirsten and generally making friends with her. A cynical observer might have said she was lulling Kirsten into a false sense of security while she made a renewed play for Jan.

100

'Hiya, gang,' she said now, 'I brought me two pals to join in the fun.'

'Flippin' heck, Donna,' Nicola said. 'You'll be staying with them next.'

Donna gave her a look of total innocence.

'We're having fun together. What's wrong with that?'

Nicola felt she needed to score a point or two on her own account.

'After the competition,' she said, 'I'm going to find this boy called Paul. I met him here last time.'

'Not another bloke you've picked up, Dobson?' Donna said disdainfully.

'No, he's not. This one was handing out leaflets for The Greenhouse Group. They're into ecology and stopping pollution.'

'Bo-ring,' Donna said. 'Is he good-looking?'

'I suppose so. But that's not the point.'

'What is then?' Donna demanded.

'I too am interested in these things,' Jan said. 'I would like to come with you, Nicola.'

'Great,' Donna said grimly. 'We'll all go.'

An hour later most of the crowd were gathered in the judging hall, waiting for the judge to make up his mind from the bizarre array of vegetable monstrosities set out along the back. Discreetly, hardly noticed by anyone, Carl was moving among the young crowd, selling cigarettes.

As the judge was making the announcement for third and second prizes, Carl moved up to Debbie, who was standing a little apart from Geoff and her grandmother. He held out a cigarette packet to her. Debbie told him to go away. Carl whispered that they were half the shop price. She told him she didn't smoke.

'Don't you want to be a big girl?' he murmured, glancing over his shoulder. 'Big girls smoke.'

Debbie insisted that big girl or not, she didn't smoke.

101

Carl told her to suit herself. He wandered off into the crowd.

Donna, Nicola, Jan and Kirsten came into the hall eating ice creams. As they approached the kids from Byker Grove, Donna pointed into the crowd.

'Nicola,' she said, 'isn't that our old maths teacher?'

'Where?'

'There.'

Donna jabbed her hand forward and struck Kirsten's. The ice cream went right down the front of Kirsten's dress. Donna immediately overflowed with apologies. She begged Kirsten to forgive her as she dabbed ineffectually at the ice cream with a hanky, simultaneously ignoring the funny look Nicola was giving her.

Excitement mounted as the judge prepared to announce the winner of the first prize. Duncan spotted Winston arriving and waved him across.

'You cut it a bit fine, didn't you?'

'No one bothered to tell me it was blimmin' happening, did they?' Winston blustered. 'I had to turn up at the Grove and hear it from Alison.'

The judge raised his hand and the crowd fell silent.

'And the first prize,' he said, 'for these splendidly gigantic leeks, goes to Byker Grove.'

Amid a riot of cheering Mary eased forward through the crowd and told Winston to go up and collect the trophy.

'You won it for us, after all.'

Reluctantly Winston went forward, took the cup and came back, trying to avoid the pats on the back and the proffered handshakes.

Meanwhile, in a corner, Debbie was excitedly telling Kelly that she had been offered cigarettes. Kelly wasn't impressed. Smoking, she said, was stupid. Debbie said it wasn't. Amanda Curtiss did it. So who was Amanda Curtiss, Kelly asked.

'She's in the sixth form and really pretty and she's got big boobs and a boyfriend who picks her up in his Spitfire.'

'Just because she smokes, doesn't mean you have to,' Kelly said.

'But it makes her look dead grown up and sophisticated. I've seen her.'

Over in the crowd from the Grove, Winston was still being congratulated and slapped on the back.

'Denton Burn'll hate us for this,' Jemma said. 'I can't wait to see their faces.'

'Yeah,' Duncan nodded, 'the man's a hero.'

He turned and slapped Winston on the back.

'Leave off, will you?' Winston snapped.

'We should put you on our shoulders and carry you through the streets like they do in films,' Jemma said, favouring Winston with a big adoring smile.

'Stop going on about it,' he growled. 'I only won a piddlin' competition, not the World Cup.'

A short distance away Debbie was running through the crowd, trying to catch up with the shifty Carl. When she finally got to him she tapped him on the back. He spun round.

'Changed me mind,' she told him.

Smirking, Carl handed her a packet of cigarettes and told her that would be eighty pence.

'I only want one,' she said.

'Don't be stupid, kid. One's not worth me while even opening the pack.'

'Please,' Debbie whined, holding out twenty pence.

Carl sighed.

'Seeing it's you,' he said, opening the packet and removing a single cigarette. 'But if you like it, you buy the rest of the pack, right?'

Debbie took the cigarette and told him she needed matches too. Carl handed her a box from his pocket.

'Anything else while you're at it?' he enquired acidly, pocketing the twenty pence.

* * *

Nicola led Donna, Jan and Kirsten up to the stand being operated by The Greenhouse Group. Paul was finishing talking to a young couple. He thanked them for joining and reminded them, as they moved away, that the more of them there were, the bigger the difference they would make.

'Hi,' Nicola said, a little embarrassed. 'It's me again.'

'Hello, you.'

'I said I'd come back and find out more about your organisation, so here I am.'

Paul told her he was glad she did, and asked what her name was.

'Nicola. These are my friends – Donna, Jan and Kirsten.'

Paul introduced himself then made a suggestion that took them all a little by surprise.

'How do you all fancy a train ride?' he said. 'I'm dying for a break.'

Within two minutes they were queuing up for the train. When they reached the head of the queue Paul got into a seat with Nicola. Donna managed to man-oeuvre it so she was sitting in another with Jan. Two strangers sat in front of Jan and Donna, so Kirsten was separated from them, sitting on her own.

'Don't mind if I pinch your boyfriend, do you, Kirsten?' Donna called out, metallically bright. 'It's only for one ride.'

'No, that's fine,' Kirsten called back, obviously put out by what had happened.

Nicola meanwhile was leaning close to Paul. She told him she had read his leaflet. She said it was awful to

104

think of all those gases floating in the atmosphere, trapping the heat. She said she felt as if she was being suffocated as she read about it. Paul said that was good. He didn't mean to be cruel, but the leaflet *was* supposed to have an impact.

'You see,' he said, 'groups like ours are so important. The more people like you become aware of how vital these issues are, the more power we have to lobby the government and industry.'

'If we know what's causing global warming,' Nicola said, 'why don't we just stop using the things that do it?'

Paul laughed gently. He said he wished it was that simple.

'But we live in a commercial world, where lots of people earn their living from the very things that create the problem.'

'Well, they should stop and do something else,' Nicola said flatly. 'It's disgusting that we know the damage we're causing, but we still carry on doing it.'

Paul looked at her, impressed with her fervour. She was looking at him with just as much admiration.

'You're really concerned about all this,' she said, 'aren't you?'

'Passionately,' Paul assured her. 'I hope you don't find it too boring.'

'No, not at all. It's the most interesting conversation I've had in ages.'

They smiled at each other.

Donna, meanwhile, was telling Jan she was glad he had come back again. She said it gave them a chance to be mates. Jan assured her he was happy to be her mate.

'Maybe I can come over and visit you and Kirsten,' she suggested. 'You were always going to show us round.'

'It would be a pleasure,' Jan said, then to Kirsten he shouted, 'Sweetheart, I was saying to Donna, we would be happy to show her round Copenhagen, wouldn't we?'

'Yes, of course,' Kirsten called back, looking as fed up as anyone could.

'That's settled, then.' Donna grinned at Jan. 'I'm coming.'

* * *

In a corner behind a group of very tall shrubs, Debbie lit her cigarette while Kelly stood by and watched.

'I think you're stupid, Debbie.'

'I'll just have one puff, to see what it's like.'

'That's what they all say,' Kelly warned darkly. 'Then they get hooked and can't stop.'

Not from one puff, Debbie said. Yes, from one puff, Kelly insisted.

Debbie took a puff and immediately started coughing. Her face turned scarlet and her eyes watered.

'So what do you think?' Kelly asked her.

'It's all right,' Debbie said, still coughing.

'You didn't inhale, though. You're supposed to blow smoke out through your nose.'

'How do you know, if you've never done it?'

'I've watched people.'

Debbie tried again but this time she nearly choked on a spasm as incoming smoke collided with an outgoing cough somewhere at the back of her throat. She was still gasping for breath when the leaves of the shrubs were pushed aside and Mary O'Malley appeared. Debbie tried to hide the cigarette behind her back.

'What's up with you, our Debbie?' Mary demanded.

'Frog in my throat, Gran,' Debbie gasped.

Mary dragged her hand from behind her back and glared at the cigarette.

'You stupid little girl!'

'I only had one puff.'

'I don't care how many you had. Those things are evil wicked poison.'

'It's just a cigarette,' Debbie moaned.

Mary snatched it away. She turned to Kelly and said she hoped she hadn't been stupid enough to try smoking. Kelly shook her head and told Mary, honestly, that she didn't like smoking.

'And neither will you, young lady,' Mary said, turning back to Debbie. 'Not by the time I've finished with you.'

Debbie begged her not to tell her dad. Anything but that, she pleaded.

'On one condition,' Mary said.

'What?'

'You're going to eat this cigarette, every last bit of it. That'll teach you never to go near them again.'

Debbie stared at her grandmother. She couldn't believe she was serious, even though she looked *deadly* serious.

'*Eat* it? You're having me on!'

Mary handed her the cigarette.

'Do you want me to tell your dad?'

Resigned and frightened at the same time, Debbie took the cigarette. Kelly looked on, horrified.

* * *

The repercussions rattled the Dobsons' house for most of Saturday night and all day Sunday. On Monday morning, as the girls prepared to leave for School, Kath was seized by another wave of anger. As soon as she got Mary alone in the living room, she started on her.

'You had no right!' Kath screeched. 'No right at all!'

'She was being a stupid girl,' Mary said, stubbornly folding her arms. 'She deserved it.'

That, Kath pointed out sharply, was not for Mary to decide.

Debbie popped her head round the door and told her

107

mother, weakly, that she was off now. Kath asked if she was sure she felt better.

'Yes,' Debbie said, wringing the most from her mother's sympathy. 'I've stopped being sick. And my tummy's only a bit funny.'

She left the house, then hurried along the front so she could listen at the living room window. Mary was saying she couldn't understand what Kath was so fussed about. She should be grateful – Debbie wasn't likely to go near cigarettes again.

'Listen, Ma,' Kath said firmly, '*I* decide how to bring Debbie up. I don't want you interfering again with your awful Victorian methods. Is that clear?'

Mary didn't like her methods being called Victorian.

'They're more like good common sense, if you ask me.'

'I'm not asking you. I'm telling you. You gave me all sorts of rotten punishments when I was a kid. I'm not having you do the same to my daughter.'

'Right,' Mary said, going off into a huff. 'If that's the way you feel, next time I'll just stand by and let her get on with it.'

'You do that, Mother. You do that.'

* * *

Gill had been at work approximately an hour when Ronnie came across the workshop. He put his hand on Gill's shoulder.

'Something funny's going on here,' he said confidentially. 'See that car?' He pointed to the one Gill and Winston had the nightmare ride in. 'It were brought in for a respray job as well as an engine overhaul. Now Bob goes to do the respray and discovers it's already been done. Know anything about it?'

Gill, feeling as if 'guilty' was stamped all over him, stared dumbly at Ronnie and shook his head.

108

CHAPTER FIVE

As Charlie left her house first thing on Wednesday morning she found PJ leaning on the wall outside. When she asked him what he was doing there he smiled and said he was just passing. Charlie smiled back.

'You're a rotten liar,' she said. 'You live on the other side of town.'

He told her he had decided to take the scenic route to school.

'You coming to the Grove tonight?' he asked.

'No,' Charlie said, shaking her head firmly.

'I'll re-phrase that. You're coming to the Grove tonight.'

Charlie insisted she wasn't. Things were bad enough without her having to put up with a load of hassle from the crowd at the Grove.

'Have I given you any hassle?' PJ asked her.

'No, you've been very sweet.'

Sweet was not his all-time favourite word, he said, but he would put up with it for now. The thing he needed to know was, had Charlie definitely made up her mind she wasn't going back to Byker Grove? Definitely, she said. She wouldn't give them the satisfaction of sending her up. Especially that Donna Bell.

'And you're not going back to Denton Burn, either?'

'No way.'

'Rettega wins all round, then,' PJ said.

'What do you mean?'

'He's put the mockers on your career, now he's putting it on your social life as well. No record, no friends, no nothing. Man, he's certainly done a number on you.'

The morning began just as gloomily for Gill. He had slept badly and woke up with a stiff neck. What with the physical pain and the permanent worry about the hit-and-run victim, he felt too low and edgy to eat breakfast. He had half a cup of coffee instead then set off down the stairs. He had just reached the front door when a hand landed on his shoulder. He nearly leapt in the air.

'My, my, we *are* a little bundle of nerves,' Carl said with an oily smile.

Gill told him, loudly and very clearly, that he was a stupid great pillock. That didn't seem to upset Carl. He went on smiling, looking Gill up and down, taking in his nervous condition.

'Something's making us very jumpy these days.'

'Yeah – it's having gruesome gorillas like you around.'

Carl put himself into the doorway, blocking Gill's way out. The real trouble, he said, was something Gill and his shrimpy little sidekick had cooked up.

'Going to give us the griff, are you?'

'Are *you* going to move away from that door?'

Carl stepped aside and opened the door. Gill was too unsettled to exchange hard looks. He swept out through the doorway and down the path.

'Better not be late for work, eh, sonny?' Carl taunted after him. 'And don't worry – whatever it is you're up to, I'll find out. I always do.'

Gill had only been at work a short time when more potential trouble descended on him, in the shape of the boss, Mr Fletcher. He interruped Gill in the middle of a job.

'Ronnie told me about the respray on that car,' he said.

Gill nodded, not quite able to look Fletcher in the eye.

'He says you don't know anything but it.'

'I don't, Mr Fletcher. It's a mystery to me.'

'Yeah.' Fletcher looked hard at Gill, as if he was trying to read something written on his face. 'It's a mystery to us, too. A car comes in for an engine tuning and a paint

110

job. The paint job gets done – pretty badly – and nobody here knows a thing. What do you reckon it was, Gillespie? Fairies come in at night, did they?'

Again Gill denied any knowledge of the mysterious paint job.

'You worked on the car.'

'Only changed the oil filter, did a tune-up, one or two other odds and ends. Painting's something I know nothing about.'

'You didn't notice anything funny about the bodywork at all?'

'Sorry,' Gill said.

Fletcher said he would leave it for now. He would talk to some of the other lads later. Somebody had to know something.

Gill returned to his work, sweating heavily, trying to remember what it was like to be carefree.

* * *

Winston turned up at the garage during the lunch break and waited by the gate. As soon as Gill came out he asked if there was any news. None, Winston said. There had been nothing else in the paper. Gill suggested it might be an idea if Winston went down to the Infirmary again.

'No chance.' Winston looked amazed that Gill could even suggest it. 'It's your turn. You could make out you're his nephew or something.'

'They'd never buy that,' Gill said. 'They'd ask questions.'

'So what are we going to do?'

'Wait.'

For what? Winston asked. Until the man croaked?

'They'll really come streaming after us then,' he said, his face clouding as he imagined it.

111

'He won't croak,' Gill said. It sounded a lot more like a hope than a certainty. 'Anyway, how can they come after us? They don't know who we are.'

'Not yet, they don't.' Winston had a persistent belief that the authorities could pinpoint anybody they wanted, if they needed to badly enough. 'I was going to ask me old man what to do,' he said.

Gill's jaw dropped.

'You never flaming told *him*?'

'No. But I wanted to. It's like being in some blimmin' horror video. It's worse. What are we going to *do*, Gill, man?'

In the meantime another conflict was developing across town, although not so dramatic as the one in which Gill and Winston found themselves. In Jan's room, Kirsten was telling him that she was having serious misgivings about Donna. Jan was surprised. He said he thought Kirsten liked Donna.

'I did, at first,' Kirsten said. 'Now I am not so sure. We are never on our own. Everywhere we go, Donna is there too.'

Jan reminded her they would be on their own when they went home. Kirsten said she wished that would be tomorrow instead of next week.

'Donna is downstairs waiting,' Jan said. 'Do you want me to tell her to go away?'

'No, no.' Kirsten frowned. 'You can't do that, it would be – '

She broke off suddenly as Donna appeared in the open doorway.

'Hiya,' she said brightly. 'Did Jan tell you? I'm taking you out for tea, my treat. To make up for spilling that ice cream on you. And I won't take no for an answer.'

Smiling wanly, Kirsten picked up her things and went to the door with Jan. Donna promptly put herself between them and linked arms as they set off briskly for the street.

Tea turned out to be a stressful affair. Donna seemed determined to kill her guests with kindness. Rather than a period of polite conversation accompanied by the tinkle of good china and the discreet nibbling of pastries, the event threatened to turn into an endurance test. Jan and Kirsten kept complaining that they couldn't eat any more, but the more they protested the harder Donna insisted. Kirsten finally became firm as Donna tried to force the last éclair on her.

'I couldn't,' she said, pushing the plate away. 'Donna, you will have me going home like Miss Piggy.'

'You don't look a bit like a pig, does she, Jan? I wish *I* looked half as gorgeous as she does.'

Jan gallantly told Donna that she was also very attractive. The remark drew a little scowl from Kirsten.

'Yeah,' Donna said, 'but boys always go for blondes. Mind you I was reading about Madonna, how her hair's all falling out because of her always bleaching it . . . '

'My hair is not bleached,' Kirsten said indignantly.

'Oh, I *know*,' Donna crooned. 'Lisa – she's my new stepmother – she's a natural blonde as well. But she says blondes fade quicker, you have to keep putting rinses on when you get older, or it looks dead yucky.'

Jan said he didn't think Kirsten would have to worry about that for a long time, since she wasn't even seventeen yet. Donna hung on to her smile with a little more difficulty now.

'That reminds me,' she said. 'On Saturday we're going out shopping again. Just us girls.'

Kirsten said she couldn't make it on Saturday. She and Jan were going to Durham to visit the cathedral.

Donna waved the objection aside.

'You can go looking round old churches another day. I'm taking you out to buy your birthday present.'

'It's not my birthday till next month!' Kirsten said, trying not to sound too exasperated.

'But you won't be here then,' Donna reminded her. 'I want to get you something now, to take back with you. Something to remind you of the smashing time we've all had together.'

* * *

Kelly spotted Carl, lurking as usual, as she made her way along the path to the Grove. She pushed her way into the bushes and collared him.

'You had no right to give Debbie cigarettes,' she told him sternly.

It wasn't cigarettes, he pointed out. It was only one.

'You still had no right.'

Carl couldn't see any fault in what he had done. The kid had asked him for the cigarette, after all. Kelly told him that was no excuse; Debbie was only thirteen, and what was more, she had got into a great deal of trouble because she took a couple of puffs.

'Did her a favour then, didn't I. Taught her a lesson.'

Kelly studied Carl with an expression of distaste.

'I don't know how you can *be* so horrible,' she said.

Carl didn't appear to be offended. In fact he smiled.

'I can be right nice, too,' he said. 'I can pay for pictures and stuff for kids who give me info.'

Kelly's eyes narrowed suspiciously behind her big glasses.

'What sort of info?'

Carl stepped closer, lowering his voice.

'That little mate of yours,' he said. 'Winston. And his oppo, Gill. Any idea what they're up to?'

'What makes you think they're up to something?'

114

Carl tapped the side of his nose.

'Anyway,' Kelly said, scowling at him, 'even if I did know anything, I wouldn't tell *you*.'

'Oh, I think you would, little one.'

Kelly threw him her most disgusted look and strode away.

Just then, at the side of the house, two rough looking lads called Kevin and Stobbo were digging holes for fence posts. Nicola stopped and watched them for a minute. Then she turned to Jemma and Duncan, who had been there when she arrived, and asked what the digging was in aid of.

'They're making a paddock for Rosie,' Duncan said.

Jemma added, with a big grin, that Brad was taking them to get the horse that evening. Nicola wasn't impressed. She said she didn't know what they wanted a mangy old horse for in the first place. She and Gwen, a part-time member of the club staff who was also a keen conservationist, had wanted that piece of ground for an organic garden.

'Well, you can't have it,' Jemma said, 'because we baggsed it first.'

'Who the heck are those two, anyway?' Nicola said.

'They painted rude words all over the monument and things,' Jemma said, 'so they're forced to do complimentary service.'

'Community service, you wally,' Duncan said.

'Anyway,' Jemma went on, 'it's a punishment and they're made to do useful things one day a week. It's a bit like being sent to prison.'

Hearing that, the one called Kevin stopped digging and glared at Jemma.

'It's no such piggin' thing,' he said.

'So why is that man supervising you all the time then?' Jemma demanded. She turned to Nicola and explained the supervisor had gone for a wee.

'Just naff off, worm,' Kevin bawled. 'You're giving us earache.'

'Don't you speak to her like that!' Nicola told him. When she looked hard at Kevin, a distant bell rang. 'Haven't I seen you somewhere before?' she said.

* * *

Clutching the bunch of flowers she had brought for her mother, Spuggie sat studying the posters in the hospital waiting room. They were all pictures of different Northumbrian beauty spots. She reckoned she could identify them all.

'That's the Farne Islands,' she told Fraser, pointing. 'We went with Gwen. And that's Whitley Bay. I remember when Mam took us there.'

'You were only about five,' Fraser said.

'Yes, but I remember it.' Spuggie looked at Fraser suddenly. 'How do you think she'll be?'

Fraser shrugged.

'I don't know, do I?'

'Do you think she'll be better?'

'I hope so,' he said.

'Will she be coming home soon?'

'Spug, I'm not the blimmin' doctor.'

The anxiety was a continuous pain for both of them. They lived with the helpless knowledge that their love and concern weren't enough to keep their mother well. Even medicine and the tender care of doctors and nurses weren't adequate; their mam was very ill, and at times Spuggie would wake up frightened in the dead of night, and she would murmur a prayer for her mother's safety. Fraser worried and fretted as much as his sister. He just didn't let it show as much.

Spuggie had thought of something else to ask when

a nurse appeared and told them they could come in now. They followed her into the ward.

Their mother looked small and fearfully thin against the pillows supporting her head and shoulders. She smiled as they kissed her in turn.

'I brought you these, Mam,' Spuggie said, holding up the flowers.

'Thanks, pet, they're lovely.'

Fraser was watching his mother, seeing how much thinner her neck had become, how frail and bony her hands. Last time he hadn't noticed how her teeth seemed to protrude, as if they had grown a little too large for her mouth. He asked her how she was feeling.

'A lot better, lovie,' she said, not meeting their eyes for a moment. 'How are you doing, more to the point?'

Fraser told her they were fine.

'But it's not like being with you,' Spuggie said.

'Yes, well, I'm afraid you'll have to put up with it a bit longer, Kirstie, pet.'

Spuggie's face became very sad.

'Are you not coming home, then?'

'Not for a while, no.'

'But you told us you were feeling better,' Fraser said huskily.

'I am. But they say I've still a long way to go. Mind you, I'll get better all the faster for knowing you two are not fretting.'

'Oh, we're not,' Spuggie said, desperately bright now. 'Honest, Mam. We're much too busy, aren't we, Frase?'

He nodded.

'We gave a birthday party for Mrs O'Malley,' he said.

'And we went to the Garden Festival with the Grove,' Spuggie put in.

'We won the giant veg competition with our leeks . . .'

'And we're going on all sorts of trips,' Spuggie said. 'We're going to Whitley Bay.'

117

Fraser looked at her.

'When are we?'

'Saturday.'

'I used to love going to Whitley Bay,' their mother said, sighing. 'When you two were little, that was. Have a grand time, the both of you.'

She closed her eyes, exhausted from the small effort of speaking. Spuggie and Fraser looked at each other, trying not to let their worry show, nor their fear.

* * *

In the main room at the Grove Nicola was telling Gwen about the two lads making the paddock in the grounds.

'They're the two we saw at Bamburgh,' she said. 'You told them off for writing on the castle walls and they sprayed you with green paint.'

'Oh, yes,' Gwen said, nodding. 'A real pair of charmers. What are they doing here?'

Nicola explained about their community service, and about Geoff detailing them to dig post holes for the paddock. Gwen thought that was a good idea, given that the ground was as hard as iron. Nicola said she still wished they could have had that stretch to grow things on, and Gwen agreed. It was Gwen who first fired Nicola's concern for the ecology and encouraged her pursuit of a healthier way of life.

'Paul said he'd help us with the garden,' Nicola said.

'Are you still seeing him?'

'When he's got time. He's awfully busy with his Greenhouse Group.'

'Don't knock it,' Gwen said. 'He's doing a great job.'

PJ came in and looked around.

'OK,' he called, raising his arms, 'cool it, everybody. A bit of hush while I make an announcement.'

Debbie said he sounded just like Philip Schofield.

Jemma said he wasn't as good-looking. Debbie took exception to that. She told Jemma to shut up and nodded to PJ to carry on.

'It's about Charlie,' PJ said.

'That prat,' Debbie snapped. 'What about her?'

'There's been a bit of a hitch with her record.'

Debbie frowned suspiciously. What sort of a hitch, she wanted to know.

'What do you mean, what sort of a hitch? A *hitch*.'

'Big hitch?' Debbie persisted. 'Medium hitch?'

'Titchy hitch?' Jemma suggested.

'It doesn't matter,' PJ said. 'But there's something I want to ask you all to do . . .'

Alison, meantime, was making sandwiches in the kitchen when Spuggie came hurtling in, followed by Fraser. She tried to shut the door on him but he forced it open and stood red-faced and panting, confronting her.

'Oh, bog off, Fraser!'

'I demand to know!' he yelled. 'What did you have to go telling her stories for?'

'Just shut up.' Spuggie was close to tears. 'I'm sick of you always bossing us.'

Alison decided she should intervene. She asked what was going on.

'We went to see me mam,' Spuggie said. 'She's not coming home for ages yet.'

'Yes,' Fraser said, glaring at his sister, 'and stupid Spuggie only told her we're going to Whitley Bay on Saturday.'

Alison said she couldn't see anything wrong with that.

'It's not true,' Fraser said.

Spuggie shut her eyes tightly for a second, as if her brother's stupidity was just too much to withstand. She opened them again and glared at him.

'She said she'll get better quicker if she's not fretting over us.'

'You still didn't have to tell her blimmin' *lies*,' Fraser said. 'What happens when she asks us what we did? Have to tell her more lies then, won't we?'

'They needn't be lies,' Alison said.

Spuggie and Fraser looked at her.

'It's my day off on Saturday. Brad's taking me out.' She winked. 'It's ages since I've been to Whitley Bay.'

'And we could come with you?' Spuggie ran forward and hugged Alison. 'Frase! Isn't that brilliant?'

'Yes, it is,' he said, nodding vigorously. 'Can I bring Joanne?'

The smile vanished from Spuggie's face.

'Why does she have to come?'

'*Can* I bring her, Alison?'

'I don't see why not,' Alison said.

Out in the grounds, Kelly had spent five minutes trying to convince Winston that, for one thing, he had been going around being so miserable that he obviously needed to confide in somebody – and for another thing, he could trust her with any secret he might decide to share.

'How do I *know* I can trust you?'

'Let's not go through all that again, Winston. We're friends, that's how you know.'

'It doesn't always follow,' Winston said gloomily. 'Sometimes friends can cause you more trouble than blimmin' *enemies*.'

'All right . . . ' Kelly spread her hands. 'If you don't want to tell me, it's no skin off my nose. Only like I said, you look so miserable lately I just thought it might help.'

She turned to walk away.

'Kelly . . . '

She stopped.

'All right,' Winston said. 'I *do* want to tell you. Only you've to promise not to say a word to nobody. Nobody at all.'

'Cross my heart and hope to die,' Kelly said.

'Right.'

Winston led her away to a private spot where, at long last, he could share his terrible secret.

* * *

The kids in the main room looked round as Charlie entered. She looked at them all in turn, seeing the expectation in their faces.

'Well,' she said, 'I suppose you've heard the news by now?'

'About your record?' Nicola said. 'Yes, we have.'

Charlie squared her shoulders.

'Well go on, then.'

'Go on what?' Duncan asked.

'Have a good laugh. I know you're all dying to, because I made a flippin' great nana of myself.'

'But you didn't,' Fraser said. 'If anyone messed up, it was that Steve What's-his-face.'

'How do you make that out?' Charlie said.

'When other artistes get to know he pulls dirty stunts like that,' PJ said, 'they'll not want to go within a mile of him, will they?'

'*I* wouldn't go to him,' Spuggie said.

'*You* can't sing,' Duncan pointed out.

'That's not the point.'

Nicola came forward. She told Charlie she had given it her best shot. It wasn't her fault Rettega was a slimeball.

'Scumbag,' Speedy said.

'Gumboil,' Jemma piped.

PJ went forward and put his hand on Charlie's shoulder. It was just as he had told her, he said. They were all on her side.

'I don't suppose you had anything to do with it?'

'Me?' PJ said. 'Of course not.'

121

Charlie told him he was still a rotten liar. She kissed him lightly and thanked him.

'Look at her,' Debbie muttered to Jemma. 'Still carrying on like she's a star.'

Nicola, behind Debbie, leaned very close and spoke near her ear.

'I'd watch it if I were you, little sister. Especially if you ever want to borrow my purple bum bag again.'

Winston and Kelly came in. Winston didn't look as tense or moody as he had before.

'I'm glad I told you,' he muttered to Kelly. 'I feel tons better.'

Kelly said *she* didn't. She looked like someone who had been given terrible news. As they sat down together she told Winston he was in real trouble.

'Tell us something we don't already know.'

'How about talking to Geoff?' Kelly suggested.

'How about chucking meself under a Metro train? It'd be quicker. And less painful.'

At that moment Geoff came in.

'Denton Burn,' he said loudly.

Everybody stared at him.

'I reckon it's time we showed 'em which club's the champions.'

'How are we going to do that?' PJ asked. 'Challenge them to a tiddly-winks match?'

'Football,' Geoff said.

'We've played them two years on the trot,' Fraser said. 'They annihilated us.'

'Both times,' Duncan added.

Geoff stood his ground, his confidence unwavering.

'Third time lucky, then,' he said.

'How do you make that out?' Winston said. 'We've still got the same lousy team.'

PJ pointed out that Winston wasn't in the team. That's why it was lousy, Winston told him.

'This time,' Geoff said, 'I've got somebody to give us some tips.'

'Who's that?' Fraser asked.

'Just a bloke that knows a bit about the game. He's popping in on Saturday afternoon.'

'Wasting his time, man,' Winston grumbled.

'Winston's right, for once,' Charlie said. 'We don't want to give that Denton Burn crowd a *third* chance to rub our noses in it.'

Geoff sighed. He looked round the room, shaking his head sadly.

'I'm sorry,' he said. 'If I'd known you felt like that, I wouldn't have rung Ken.'

'Who's Ken?' Debbie asked.

'My oppo at Denton Burn. I told him we'd be happy to take them on, a week on Saturday. So . . . ' He looked round the room again. 'I'm afraid we're stuck with it.'

*   *   *

Alison was attending to club paperwork when Brad put his head into the office. He asked if she was looking forward to the weekend and their first date. She reminded him it wasn't their first. Very well, Brad conceded, their first *official* date. Where did she fancy going? Maybe somewhere miles from it all, he suggested. They could stay overnight . . .

'How do you fancy Whitley Bay?' Alison said.

'Whitley Bay?' Brad thought about it. 'Bit crowded, isn't it?'

'Not really.'

Brad shrugged.

'OK. If you want Whitley Bay, Whitley Bay you shall have. Just the two of us.'

'Er, not quite.' Alison looked at him warily. 'I told Spuggie she could come. And Fraser. And Joanne.'

Brad stared at her.

'What about Speedy?' he said. 'And Winston and PJ? And Debbie and Duncan and . . . ' He tensed himself as Alison leaned across and punched him. 'It's all right,' he grunted. 'I can see how desperate you are to be alone with me.'

Alison turned serious and told Brad it was important. He told her, just as seriously, that he had guessed as much, knowing her.

Jemma and Duncan came in. They stood staring up at Brad.

'It's time to go and get her,' Jemma solemnly announced.

'Rosie,' Brad said, nodding. 'My *other* girlfriend. Come on, then. It's not polite to keep a lady waiting.'

They reached the scrap yard fifteen minutes later. Ted Boneo was waiting for them at the gate. He didn't look happy. As soon as they reached the gate he took Brad aside and whispered something to him. Brad looked shocked. He came back to where Jemma and Duncan were waiting.

'I'm afraid I've bad news,' he said. 'It's Rosie. She's dead.'

The kids looked stunned. Ted came forward, shaking his head. Brad asked him when it had happened. That morning, Ted said. One minute she had been fine, the next she keeled over. The vet had said it was her heart.

Jemma began to cry.

'It's all right, little un,' Ted said. He clicked his fingers. 'She went like that.'

Duncan looked furious.

'It's your fault,' he told Ted, 'making her work all those years, pulling that heavy cart . . . '

'All right, Duncan,' Brad said sharply. 'That's enough.'

'She was a willing worker, was Rosie,' Ted said.

'Strong as an ox. I never asked her to do what she couldn't. She just wore out, that's all. Same as me.'

They stood in awkward silence for a minute, Jemma crying softly into her hanky.

'Right, then,' Brad said, 'we'll be off, again. I'm sorry.'

'Me too,' Ted said. 'I know she was going to a good home. She'd have been happy there.'

Jemma started to sob again. Brad let her and Duncan away.

* * *

At the Grove, Kevin and Stobbo were still working on the paddock. For a while Debbie watched them from a distance, then she went across and told them they had better hurry up, the others would be back with the horse soon.

'Go and play on the motorway, kid,' Kevin said.

'You've got to do what you're told,' Debbie informed him sharply. 'It's what you're here for.'

She was about to say more, then she caught sight of Donna and ran over to her.

'Listen,' she panted, 'Donna, I've got some news for you, it's hilarious . . .'

In the main room Nicola and Charlie were talking in a corner. Nicola was asking if Charlie would try to find another producer. Charlie said she wouldn't, she was finished with all that.

'But you can't just give up on all your ambitions!'

'It's not such a big deal. And at least everyone's been nice about it, thanks to PJ.'

'What do you mean, thanks to PJ?' Nicola demanded. 'I wouldn't have had a go at you.'

'You wouldn't,' Charlie said, 'but some of them would.'

With immaculate timing Donna breezed across the room and stood in front of Charlie.

125

'Shame about your record,' she said.

'See what I mean?' Charlie said to Nicola.

Nicola turned on Debbie.

'I suppose you couldn't wait to be the bearer of bad tidings?'

Debbie's eyes widened innocently.

'Donna's disappointed. Like we all are. Not every youth club's got its very own celebrity.'

'I shouldn't worry,' Donna was saying, her arm round Charlie, 'it's probably all for the best. You've got to have charisma to be a star.'

Charlie smiled.

'At least I know I can always count on you, Donna.'

'Oh you can, pet.'

'To be totally, boringly predictable,' Charlie added, walking away.

Outside, meanwhile, Kevin and Stobbo had just heard of the death of Rosie and were giving three rousing cheers. Jemma screamed at them to shut up. She told them they were horrible, and she hoped all their teeth would drop out.

Geoff appeared, demanding to know what all the commotion was about.

'Old nag's popped her clogs, guv,' Kevin explained, grinning. 'So I reckon that lets us out.'

Geoff asked how he managed to reckon that.

'No horse, no paddock,' Stobbo said. 'Simple.'

Geoff turned and beckoned to Nicola and Gwen as they came out of the house. When they came across he asked if they still wanted this patch of ground for an organic garden.

'Yes please!' Nicola squealed.

'Absolutely,' Gwen said.

'Right,' Geoff told them, 'it's yours.'

Gwen put her hands on her hips and surveyed the ground. She said it would all need turning over first.

'And there's loads of stones and bits of rubble,' Nicola said.

Geoff nodded, taking it all in. He turned to Kevin and Stobbo.

'You heard the ladies,' he said. 'Get digging.'

'What?' Stobbo said, horrified. 'The lot, you mean?'

'Yes, the lot.' Geoff pointed to Gwen. 'And she's in charge.'

Stobbo looked insulted.

'Her?' he said. 'Little Specky Four-Eyes?'

'Whatever she says, you do.' Geoff turned to Jemma and Duncan. 'You two – office. We've things to discuss.'

'What things?' Jemma said.

'We'll still have room to keep something small,' Geoff said. 'How do you fancy rabbits?'

'Or a goat?' Duncan suggested.

'Ducks?' Jemma said.

They followed Geoff into the house. Kevin and Stobbo stood glaring at Gwen.

'Right, boys,' she said sweetly. 'Get digging. Or do I have to get out my paint spray?'

* * *

Early on Saturday morning Spuggie was in the kitchen at the Gallagher house, packing sandwiches. Fraser was doing his best to help her. At twenty minutes to nine she went to the kitchen door and yelled for Joanne, warning her that if she didn't hurry up they would be late.

'I don't know what you had to invite her for anyway. She's always a blimmin' slowcoach.'

'Put a sock in it,' Fraser said. 'We've bags of time.'

Speedy was sitting at the table, watching them. He said he wished he was going to Whitley Bay too. Fraser said he could squeeze in – Brad was borrowing a bigger car. Speedy thought about it, then said he'd better not.

He had promised Geoff he would show up at the Grove that afternoon.

'His naff pal's coming. The one that's going to tell us how to beat Denton Burn at football.'

'Geoff wanted me to come too,' Fraser said. 'But I said I'd made plans. It's a waste of time, isn't it? They'll still smash us.'

'I know,' Speedy said, nodding sadly. 'I'd much sooner come with you.'

Spuggie strode to the door and yelled to Joanne again.

'If you don't get a move on we're going without you!'

Upstairs, still in her pyjamas, Joanne was lying on her bed, avidly reading an airmail letter that had come for her ten minutes before. So far, she hadn't heard a single word Spuggie bellowed at her.

* * *

Kelly was doing some early shopping for the family. As she came out of the fruiterer's she didn't notice Carl fall into step behind her. She wasn't aware of him at all until he reached over her shoulder and whipped an apple from her bag. She turned to deliver a mouthful. When she saw who it was she turned away again and tried to walk on. Carl came with her.

'Had any more thoughts on what I asked you yesterday, kid?'

'What about?'

'Your little mate Winston. And his ugly pal Gill.'

'Go away,' Kelly said, getting frightened. 'I've told you, I don't know anything.'

Carl moved closer to her as they walked, gripping her arm tightly, almost painfully.

'What makes me think you're telling us fibs, little one?'

* * *

The sea was bigger and breezier than Spuggie remembered. Everything seemed so much cleaner and brighter than in town, too. Walking along the promenade beside Alison and Brad, she glanced at her brother and Joanne. They looked as if they were enjoying themselves, too.

Fraser had just asked Joanne if she was glad she had come. She said she was. She also told him, without being asked, that she thought Alison and Brad were very nice, and that she believed they were in love.

'Soppy girls,' Fraser grunted.

Joanne had held off from telling her news as long as she could. Now she told Fraser: at long last she'd had another letter from her brother.

'What does he say? Is it still as awful there?'

'He hates it. But he's had an interview and he says that somebody will be contacting me.'

'What for?'

'To ask me about him. They've got to be sure before they let him come.'

'You mean there's a chance they will?'

Joanne nodded, smiling.

'Fraser, I could be seeing him soon. I could soon be meeting my brother!'

The excitement suddenly exploded in her. She hugged Fraser and whirled round with him. Alison and Brad watched.

'Somebody's happy,' Alison said.

Brad looked at her.

'Think there's any chance of a hug for me?'

'I'm sure there is,' Alison said. 'Go and ask her.'

'Come here,' Brad growled.

He grabbed Alison and hugged her. Spuggie stood by, staring disdainfully at the two hugging couples, wondering why they bothered to come to the seaside, if all they were going to do was mess around like that and not even look at the sea and the sand.

In the afternoon, when they'd had their sandwiches and fizzy drinks, they walked barefoot along the beach, Brad and Alison hand in hand, Fraser and Joanne also hand in hand, with Spuggie trailing behind, splashing in the water.

After a few minutes Brad stopped suddenly and dipped his toes into the water. He nodded and turned to Alison.

'I reckon this is about as good a place as any,' he said.

'No chance. I'm not paddling in this. It's like ice.'

'Not to paddle,' Brad said. 'To ask you to marry me.'

Alison frowned.

'Are you serious?'

'No, I always joke about things like that.' He put his face closer to hers. 'Will you, Alison?'

She was still frowning.

'Why?' she said.

'Because I love you.'

The frown cleared and she smiled, a little shyly.

'I reckon that's as good a reason as any.'

'Well?' Brad said. 'Do I have to go down on one knee?'

'Not in front of the kids. You can do it later.'

'If I do, what will the answer be?'

'The same as it is now.' Alison said. 'Yes.' She let Brad grab her, but put up a hand before he kissed her. 'One thing. Let's keep it a secret, eh? Just until I've had a chance to tell Mike. I owe him that.'

They kissed by the water's edge, long and lingering, their arms tightly twined around each other.

'Are we going to get them ice creams,' Spuggie demanded loudly, 'or are you two going to stand there snogging all day?'

Brad and Alison disentangled. Brad took Spuggie's hand.

'Come on,' he said. 'Double cornets all round. To celebrate.'

'What are we celebrating?' Spuggie asked.

'We'll think of something.'

It was two-thirty. By that time, most of the soccer team were gathered in the main room at the Grove, together with the usual Saturday crowd. PJ, after looking all over the house, came across and asked Speedy where Fraser had mizzled off to.

'He's meant to be on the team, after all.'

'Gone to Whitley Bay with Alison and Brad,' Speedy said. 'Lucky pig.'

They should all have gone, Winston said, instead of wasting their time there. Jemma asked him why he thought they were wasting their time. Because, he said, Geoff's mate probably knew as much about football as she did.

'Besides,' Speedy said, 'he's probably dead old, like Geoff.'

'With a pot belly,' Debbie added.

'Geoff's not got a pot belly,' Nicola said.

'He's no lean, mean fighting machine, though,' PJ said. 'Is he?'

Kelly said she thought they were all being horrible about Geoff. It was just what he deserved, Winston said, for handing that Denton Burn lot another chance to wipe their feet on the Grove.

'I can just imagine them now,' Speedy said, 'grinning all over their stupid gobs.'

'Especially that Greg,' Charlie said, with feeling.

Winston strode across the room impatiently.

'So where is he anyway, this genius who's going to turn the world's naffest team into superstars overnight?'

As if he had been prompted, Geoff appeared in the doorway. He was smiling broadly.

'He's just arrived,' he said, raising a welcoming arm. 'Come on in, mate. Meet the gang.'

The place went silent as Geoff's mate appeared.

131

Winston gulped, then blinked. He could hardly believe his eyes. He blinked again and stared. There was no mistake. It was Paul Gascoigne. Himself. In person.

He smiled at everybody and waved.

'Hiya, kids,' he said. 'The name's Gazza.'

* * *

Gill finished waxing Mr Fletcher's car at one minute to three. It was an immaculate job, he would have defied anybody to do better. He had double-coated the paint-work, putting on a deep skin that would last through the worst kind of weather. He had buffed it to a near-flawless gloss, then examined it from every angle and removed even the tiniest smudges and flecks. In the circumstances, what with the wage rise and so forth, he felt it was the least he could do. He stood back from the car, wiping the wax from his hands with a rag as Fletcher came across from the office.

'Is she ready?'

'Absolutely, Mr Fletcher.'

Fletcher nodded approvingly.

'I appreciate you working Saturday afternoon, lad.'

Gill said it was OK, he had nothing else to do.

'Oh,' Fletcher said, on the point of going away again, 'about that mysterious respray job . . . '

Gill tried to look innocently curious.

'We've had no luck finding the culprit.'

'No?'

'No.' Fletcher sighed. 'It's a shame, because it puts everybody under suspicion.'

Gill took a deep breath.

'Mr Fletcher . . . I should have told you straight off. It was me.'

There was a moment of taut silence between them.

'Go on,' Fletcher said quietly.

'I had to move it, see. There was nobody else here. It was parked right up against the wall and I couldn't get at it to change the oil filter. It seemed OK . . . '

'Till you saw the scratch and thought you'd done it?'

'Yeah,' Gill nodded. 'So I tried to patch it up. I know it was stupid.'

Fletcher looked thoughtful for a minute.

'It *was* stupid, son. Not moving the car, though you'd no right to do that. Not even doing a clumsy respray. You know what was *really* stupid? Lying about it.'

'I'm sorry,' Gill said.

'So am I, lad. See Ronnie on Monday and get your cards.'

Gill felt like he had been punched.

'Mr Fletcher?'

'I'm an easy-going chap, son, but I've got one golden rule. Always have had. I don't employ liars.'

Fletcher walked away. Gill stared after him, feeling the fabric of his safety start to give way. This was the start, he thought. Where would it stop?

* * *

Donna and Kirsten were in a café. They had come at Donna's suggestion, because she had something to tell Kirsten. Something important.

'I'm only telling you this because I like you,' Donna said, sipping her coffee. 'I didn't expect to like you, but I do.'

'I like you too,' Kirsten said stiffly. 'What is it you want to tell me?'

'It's about me and Jan.'

Donna paused for dramatic effect, blowing on her coffee, looking around to make sure they weren't being overheard.

'You know we said we went around together when he was over here?'

Kirsten nodded.

'Well, actually, it was more than that.'

'How do you mean?' Kirsten said, frowning.

'At first, we just went out.' Donna's eyes became misty with recollection. 'We liked each other a lot. Then one day he took us to Cragside . . . '

'He took me there, too,' Kirsten said. 'It is a beautiful place.'

'I'll always remember it,' Donna sighed. Her eyelashes fluttered softly. 'It was the first time I'd ever let a boy go all the way.'

'*What*?'

'I didn't want to at first. I was scared. But Jan was so sweet, he promised nothing awful would happen, and even if it did he said he loved me and he wanted us to get married when he'd finished his studies.'

Kirsten looked horrified.

'He asked you to marry him?'

'We got engaged that day,' Donna said, her voice turning husky. 'He bought me the most beautiful ring. It was dead romantic, we had to keep it secret because my dad would have gone spare.' She sighed again. 'Only, in the end, I realised I was much too young to tie myself down. Poor Jan, he was heartbroken.'

'But it was only just after he got home that he proposed to me!'

'It was on the rebound,' Donna said gently. 'And I don't think that's very fair to you.' She smiled sadly. 'You're my friend, Kirsten. You've a right to know the truth.'

* * *

Gill got back to his house late in the evening. He had walked around for a long time, stunned, wondering

134

what to do next, fearful of what might happen without him being able to prevent it. Finally he had gone into a cinema, drawn by the notion of the protective darkness. He could only vaguely remember the film he had seen.

He went into his room and kicked the door shut behind him. He leaned on it, rubbing his eyes.

'Tut, tut,' Carl said from the other side of the room. 'Late back, aren't we?'

'What the piggin' heck . . .'

'Got ourselves another little ladyfriend, have we?'

'I've been to the blimmin' pictures, not that it's anything to do with you.'

'I let myself in while I waited,' Carl said. 'Knew you wouldn't mind.'

Gill told him that was where he was wrong. He jerked open the door again and told Carl to scram. No, Carl said, not until they had talked. Gill told him they had nothing to talk about.

'I think we have, sunshine,' Carl said. 'I think you've a very interesting story to tell me. About how you nicked a car from work and took it on a joy-ride with that little runt Winston. How you knocked a bloke down and he's on the critical list . . .'

'I'll kill him!' Gill roared.

'Don't look so worried,' Carl soothed. 'I'd never split on a mate. I always mind my own business, me.' He smiled. 'For a price.'

'What are you talking about?'

'A measly twenty quid a week will keep me mouth well-buttoned.'

'You're mad!' Gill said. 'I've not got that kind of dosh! I've just lost me blimmin' job!'

Carl sighed as he moved to the open door.

'That's your problem, sunshine,' he said. 'Twenty smackers a week. I don't care how you get it.' At the door he smiled again. 'Just get it.'

CHAPTER SIX

Donna came downstairs to the empty bar, fluffing her hair with both hands. It was early Sunday morning and she was still in her shortie nightie. Jan turned from the window as she came in.

'Lisa said you wanted us,' Donna said, smothering a yawn.

'Yes,' Jan looked anxious. 'Donna, I –'

'Couldn't you have waited till I got up? I look a fright without me mascara.'

'Donna, do you know where Kirsten is?'

She looked blank, uncomprehending.

'She has gone,' Jan said.

'Where to?'

'Who knows? She has left me a note saying she does not want to see me ever again.'

Donna blinked with elaborate innocence. 'Why would she do that?'

'I have no idea. I thought she might have said something to you.'

'No. Nothing.' Donna made a show of thinking hard. 'Maybe she's gone back to Denmark.'

'I telephoned her parents. If she was there, they would have told me.'

Perhaps, Donna suggested delicately, Kirsten had run off with someone else. Jan shook his head grimly. His Kirsten would not do that.

'Well, something's got up her nose,' Donna said. 'She's a nice girl, but she can be a bit temperamental. I shouldn't let it bother you, pet.'

Jan looked helpless. 'Do you think she will come back?'

'Of course.' Donna sidled closer, putting her hand on his arm. 'And if she doesn't, there's plenty more fish in the sea.'

Across town another early call was being made, a lot more frantically in this case, and with a possibly violent outcome. Gill was hammering on the front door at Winston's house, using the side of his fist to bash the flaking paintwork. He paused and stepped back, glaring at the upstairs windows. A curtain moved and part of Winston's face appeared. He eased up the window and poked his head out, staring at Gill bleary-eyed.

'What do you think you're doing, man?'

'Get down here!' Gill snarled.

'It's pigging eight o'clock on Sunday morning! Me dad'll go spare!'

'Just get down here, all right?'

Winston disappeared from view. A few moments later he opened the door and stood there in his pyjamas.

'What the heck is it?'

Gill grabbed him by the lapels. 'What did you have to snitch on us to that nutter Carl for?'

'I never!'

'Don't give us that. He knows.'

'About the car?'

'The accident,' Gill said. 'The hospital, everything.'

Winston eased himself out of Gill's grip. 'It wasn't me,' he said. 'I swear, it wasn't me.'

'Who was it then?' Gill stared at him hard. 'You told somebody, didn't you?' Winston's eyes wavered. He turned his head aside. 'Oh, you blimmin' little pillock! You stupid pathetic little twerp!'

Winston stared at the ground, wishing it would open and swallow him.

* * *

The following Saturday morning, as Nicola was heading

for the Byker Arms, she saw Kevin walking towards her. For once, Stobbo wasn't with him. As they drew level Nicola pointedly looked across the street.

'Too stuck up to talk to us, then?' Kevin said, stopping.

Reluctantly Nicola stopped too.

'I've got nothing to say,' she said coldly.

'Hello wouldn't hurt.'

'Hello.'

The smirk melted from Kevin's face. 'I'm not something you scrape off your shoe, you know.'

'So why do you behave like it?' Nicola demanded. 'You and your pal, everything you do is rotten. Rubbishing property, chucking cans in the sea, being foul to people – why do you take what's beautiful and make it ugly?'

'Lighten up, girl – it's just something to do.'

She scarcely had the words to tell him how much she despised him.

'If that's your idea of fun,' she said, 'then I'm sorry for you. Have you ever tried doing something positive for just once in your stupid lives? You might just find out you get an even bigger kick from it than behaving like something that crawled out of the swamp.'

Kevin blinked at her. 'You don't think a lot of me, do you?'

'If you must know, I think you're totally pathetic.'

Kevin grinned. 'No chance of a date, then?'

'I'd sooner jump from a plane without a parachute,' Nicola said, and marched away.

A few minutes later, sitting in Donna's bedroom, she delivered an edited version of what had happened.

'Blimmin' cheek,' Donna said. 'What did you say?'

'Told him what I thought of him,' Nicola said, not able to remember her exact words.

'Weren't you afraid he'd thump you?'

Nicola shook her head.

'They're just big bags of wind, that sort. Prick 'em and they pop.'

'Not like Jan,' Donna said, dreamy all of a sudden. 'He's a gentleman.'

Nicola asked if there was any news yet of Kirsten.

'I don't know. I'll ask Jan at the match.'

Nicola looked surprised. 'He won't be coming, will he?'

'Why not?'

'Donna, Kirsten's disappeared into thin air. He must be worried sick.'

'She can look after herself,' Donna said dismissively.

'But it's been nearly a week now . . .'

'She's probably having a ball,' Donna insisted.

'But *why* would she have taken off like that? They were so happy together.'

'Well . . .' Donna stared towards the window. 'Perhaps she found out something about him.'

'Like what?'

'*I* don't know, do I?' Donna waggled her head indignantly. '*I'm* not his girlfriend, am I?'

* * *

It was the biggest day any of the Byker Grove crowd could remember. The day of the showdown match with Denton Burn. In the kitchen at the Grove Alison, Winston, Kelly, Debbie and Spuggie were making sandwiches. There was cheese, cold meat, jam and margarine all over the place. They were thoroughly enjoying themselves.

Alison said she thought it was tempting fate to plan a celebration party before they had even won, but Debbie told her not to be daft – how could they lose with Gazza on their side?

Alison said she was surprised they had kept it a secret

from Denton Burn. Kelly told her they could keep secrets when they really wanted to.

'*Some* of us can, blabbermouth,' Winston said, glaring at Kelly.

'She's not told them anything,' Spuggie said.

'I'm not *talking* about blimmin' Denton Burn.'

Winston helped himself to a sandwich and walked out.

'I thought you two were friends,' Alison said. 'What have you done to upset him, pet?'

'Nothing,' Kelly said. 'Nothing I know of, anyway.'

Over at the Gallagher house, Speedy was cleaning his football boots in the kitchen. Joanne came in with the bread for the sandwiches.

'I got medium,' she told Speedy, looking round. 'They didn't have thin. Where's Mum?'

'Went out,' he said. 'Got a surprise for us, she said.'

'What?'

'Dunno. It's a surprise. She won't be back till this afternoon.'

'So who's doing lunch?'

'Me,' Speedy said. He flexed a slender biceps. 'I'm having spaghetti hoops. Gazza says pasta gives you energy.'

'Where's she gone?'

'Never said.'

'That's funny. I thought she was coming to the match.' Joanne turned and frowned at Speedy. 'And *you* shouldn't be doing that in here.'

'Mind your own business.'

Speedy gathered up the brushes and polish and put them away. He lifted his boots and was going out with them when he remembered something.

'There's a letter come for you,' he said, pointing to the mantelpiece. 'I put it on there. I did think about steaming it open. I held it up to the window to see if it was money . . .'

Joanne picked up the official-looking envelope, ignoring Speedy's chatter. She turned it in her hands a couple of times, then quickly went upstairs to read it, her excitement over the football match temporarily suspended.

* * *

The football fever hadn't reached Gill. He lay on his bed, staring at the ceiling, aware of the outside world moving and himself motionless, waiting for whatever nastiness life decided to dump on him next.

He didn't have to wait long. The door opened and Carl stepped into the room.

'Don't you ever knock?'

Carl went back to the door and knocked it twice. 'Is that better?'

'What do you want?'

'Just checking up,' Carl said. 'I'm worried about you, see.'

'Oh yes?'

'You've hardly been out of the house lately.'

'Your concern,' Gill said, still gazing at the ceiling, 'is very touching.'

Carl leaned on the wall. 'You've made no effort to get a job. Not easy that, though. Not without a reference.'

'Just bog off, will you? Leave us alone.'

'Can't do that, sunshine.' Carl came and stood by the side of the bed. 'I think I've been very patient. But it's been a week now.'

'What has?' Gill said, looking at him.

'Since I told you my price for keeping quiet about your little escapade,' Carl said. 'I can't wait forever.' He leaned forward, putting his face in Gill's line of vision. 'The first twenty quid by tomorrow, or I squeal to the fuzz. You're getting off cheap, really.'

He turned and left the room, almost soundlessly, leaving Gill with one more weight pressing on his brain.

* * *

On her way to the Grove Charlie passed Greg. She hoped he wouldn't see her, but as she drew level he spoke.

'Going to give us your autograph, superstar?'

Charlie kept on walking. Greg followed, walking alongside.

'Oh, I forgot,' he said. 'Madonna's got nothing to worry about, has she?'

Charlie shook her head. 'To think I was once insane enough to actually *like* you.'

'I liked you too, in those days. Before you got big-headed.'

'I don't need this conversation, Greg.'

'Yeah, well you've plenty on your mind, right?' He grinned maliciously. 'Last week your record producer dumped you, today your new mates are in for a hammering.'

Charlie glanced at him, saw the sickening smug look on his face.

'What makes you think you're going to hammer us?'

'Oh, come on, Charlie. Everybody knows Byker Grove's a rubbish team.' He held out his hand. 'Come back on the winning side.'

Charlie ignored his hand.

'If I were you,' she said, 'I wouldn't be too sure which side that is.'

At the Grove, everybody was ready to leave for the football ground. In the office Geoff was having a last-minute chat with Gwen.

'You're sure you don't mind stopping here on your own?' he said.

'Somebody's got to man the fort. Anyway, I've got plenty of work to do outside.'

'Right, well.' Geoff opened the door. 'Wish us luck.'

Gwen said she didn't think they were going to need it.

Spuggie and Debbie came to the door.

'Everybody's ready, Geoff,' Spuggie said, 'but Gazza's not here yet.'

'He's meeting us there,' Geoff told her.

He took both girls by the hand and they went outside, followed by Gwen. They piled into the already crammed minibus and a moment later Geoff drove off. Gwen waved until they disappeared through the gates, then she turned and went back to the house. She didn't see Kevin and Stobbo watching her.

At the football ground the two minibuses of players and supporters arrived at the same time. Both clubs piled out and straight away the Denton Burners began taunting the Grovers.

'So what's this secret weapon, then?' Greg shouted. 'Don't tell us – you're going to put Spuggie in goal.'

'No, that's not it,' somebody else called out. 'They're going to play on roller skates!'

'No, no – they've been putting castor oil on their cornflakes!'

The Denton Burners fell about as the jibes got wilder and wilder. The Byker Grovers bore it with dignity and smug fortitude. The team got themselves ready for the fray, saying nothing, passing the occasional wink from one to the other.

Fraser was lacing up his boots as Joanne came over and told him she'd had another letter. 'When?'

'This morning.'

'Why didn't you say?'

'I didn't want the others to know,' she said. 'Not yet, anyway. Superstitious, I suppose.'

Fraser asked if it was from her brother.

'No. It's from the Home Office. They're sending someone to see me. Oh Fraser . . .' She shivered with pleasure. 'It's really beginning to happen. Keep your fingers crossed for me, will you?'

'Of course I will. It's great news, Jo. Like PJ would say, it's cool, man!'

They laughed happily as a few yards away Jan approached Nicola. Nicola asked if there was any news. 'Nothing,' he said glumly.

'So what'll you do now?'

'We had our return tickets booked for later today,' Jan said. 'I will go to the ferry and pray she is on it.'

'She will be,' Nicola said, hoping she was right. 'I'm sure of it.'

Donna appeared on the edge of the crowd. She waved frantically and pushed her way to where Nicola and Jan were standing.

'See?' she said, linking her arm through Jan's. 'I told you he'd be here.'

'He's only come to say goodbye,' Nicola said.

Jan nodded. 'I am going home to Denmark.'

'Oh.' Donna's eyes narrowed. 'She's back, then, is she?'

'No. But I am hoping she will be at the ferry.'

Donna smiled tightly.

'Even if you don't make up,' she said, 'there's still the bright side.'

'What bright side?' Nicola asked.

'I can always go over to visit, like we planned,' Donna told her. 'Cheer him up, you know.' Turning to Jan she said, 'It's no fun being dumped, is it, pet?'

Greg had cornered Winston at the edge of the field.

'Admit it, titch,' he said. 'It was all just a load of your usual bull, wasn't it? There *is* no secret weapon.'

Winston's attention was elsewhere. He was watching Carl and Kelly, standing together a few yards away. Kelly was shaking her head.

'I'm *talking* to you, man,' Greg said.

Winston went on staring into the crowd. Greg gave up and walked away.

Beyond the spot where Carl and Kelly stood, Geoff stood gazing anxiously towards the gate. A small deputation – Spuggie, Fraser, Speedy, Duncan and Debbie – came across and stood in front of him.

'Where's Gazza?' Fraser asked. 'It's nearly time for the kick-off.'

'He'll not let us down,' Geoff said, his face remaining anxious. 'I'm *sure* I said I'd meet him here . . .'

* * *

Gwen was on her knees by a part of the new garden area that had been freshly dug. On the ground before her were pots of seedlings she had brought out to plant. As she sorted through them she was suddenly aware of a shadow on the ground. She looked up and saw the grinning faces of Kevin and Stobbo.

'All gone to the match, have they?' Kevin said.

'Not everybody.'

'Funny,' Stobbo said, 'we just saw 'em go. Every last one of 'em.'

Kevin nodded. 'Every one but you, Gwen, my friend. What's that short for? Gwendoline?'

Both youths seemed to find that hilarious. Kevin stooped and picked up a couple of seedlings. 'Got any more orders for us? Want us to plant these, do you?' He dropped the seedlings and stamped on them. 'Will that do?'

Gwen got to her feet. As she moved they moved, grinning, following her as she hurried back to the house. She ran into the office, terrified, and grabbed her jacket from behind the door. Snatching her handbag off the desk she fumbled out her car keys and ran back outside.

They were waiting by the door. She spun as they moved in on either side of her, grinning still, their eyes hard and malicious. Gwen backed towards her car. She got the door open and slid inside, slamming the door shut. As she tried to fit the key into the ignition they began rocking the car from side to side.

'Stop that!' Gwen shouted at them. 'Just stop it! You'll be in even worse trouble . . .'

Suddenly, inexplicably, both youths' faces were pressed against the windshield, their features distorted. As Gwen stared, two powerful hands grabbed the pair and jerked them away from the car. Finally she could see what was happening – Gazza had arrived, and he was attending to the emergency with his usual skill and energy.

When he had frog-marched Kevin and Stobbo to the path he delivered a terse, stern lecture. Gwen couldn't hear what was said, but after a few seconds she saw the two lads slink away. Gazza came back to the car.

'I don't think they'll be bothering you again, love.' He looked around him. 'Where is everyone?'

'Gone to the match,' Gwen said.

Gazza opened the passenger door and jumped in.

'Right then,' he said, grinning. 'Can you put your foot down?'

* * *

A van had arrived at the football ground. Lou Gallagher got out along with the driver. They went to the back and opened the doors, then Lou operated an electric hoist. In the crowd, Charlie was the first to notice what was happening.

'Robert!' she yelled, running across the grass. A lot of the other kids followed her. She got to the van as Robert's wheelchair touched the ground. 'Oh, Robert! When did they let you out?'

146

'This morning,' he said, grinning. 'It was meant to be a surprise.'

'It certainly is!' Charlie said. 'It's brilliant!'

The kids crowded round the wheelchair.

'Are you out for good?' Joanne asked him.

'As long as he behaves himself,' Lou said.

'And are you going to be able to walk?' Spuggie said.

Robert said he had been told he was now back to just about where he was before the fall.

'So eventually, with any luck . . .'

'Well I'm really glad to see you,' Speedy said, blinking back a couple of tears. 'Isn't it great that Robert's back, PJ?'

'Yeah,' PJ said, glancing at Charlie, seeing the adoring way she looked at Robert. 'It's really fantastic.'

As the kids milled around Robert's wheelchair Alison was leaning on the barrier, watching them. She turned as somebody touched her hand. It was Mike, her former boyfriend.

'What are you doing here?'

'Keeping up an old tradition,' he said. 'I always supported Byker Grove.'

'Yes, you always did.'

'And I knew I'd see you here.'

It was strange, Alison thought, how two people who had been really close could seem like strangers so quickly. Mike was like someone from the distant past – and only an acquaintance, at that.

'It's been a couple of weeks since you moved out, Ali. You said you needed some space to think things through.'

And he had been so understanding about that, she thought. He hadn't complained at the time she told him, and he hadn't tried to contact her until now. He had been a perfect gentleman in circumstances that couldn't have been easy for him.

'Has it helped,' he said, 'having this time to think things over?'

'Yes. I should have told you. I was going to. I've been a coward about it.'

Mike's eyes turned sad. 'You're not coming back.'

'It's over, Mike. I'm going to marry Brad.'

She watched him take it in. He had never been afraid to face anything, he would start to live with this straight away. He smiled.

'Good luck, love. Looks like the best man won, eh? Tell him to take care of you, from me.'

Alison knew if she said anything she would cry. In silence she watched Mike walk away.

On the edge of the field Greg was complaining loudly that the stalling time was over. Speedy and Winston were hopping from foot to foot, watching the gates, wondering if they had been let down.

'Where the heck *is* he?' Winston groaned.

Gwen's car came bowling through the gates and drew up with squealing brakes at the end of the pitch.

'Here it is,' Greg yelled. 'Their famous secret weapon finally arrives! And guess what, folks – it's a computerised football space module!'

There was more jeering as Gwen got out of the car. Then Gazza stepped out. Silence fell.

Gazza went across to Geoff. 'Sorry I'm late, mate. But you said to meet you at the Grove.'

Geoff slapped himself on the forehead.

'Just as well you did, as it happens,' Gazza murmured. 'Now I'm here, shall we get this show on the road?'

For a minute the Denton Burners stood looking at one another.

'I don't care if Superman arrived,' Greg said defiantly. 'He couldn't make up for this outfit.' He crossed to Geoff, grinning. 'Imagine, we'll be able to say we whopped Paul Gascoigne's team.'

His grin faded as Geoff and Gazza began heading for the Athletic Club Hall.

'Where are we playing then?' Greg demanded.

'Follow me and you'll find out,' Geoff said.

Inside, the press were assembled for the big event – a Subbuteo match between Byker Grove and Denton Burn. Greg insisted it was a fiddle, but Geoff reminded him of the conditions.

'Any game we choose, that was the agreement. And we chose this one.'

It was an exciting game as table-top matches go, largely because Gazza was as talented at the Subbuteo board as he was on the field. Byker Grove won a resounding victory, the press took pictures and there was a grand presentation.

Later, when it was all over, Donna, Nicola and Jan stood together and watched the Denton Burn minibus drive past them and out through the gate.

'Good,' Donna said. 'That's sorted *them* out with knobs on. Come on Jan, we're all going back to the Grove for a party.'

'No,' Jan said, shaking his head, 'I must get to the ferry early. Please hope for me that she is there.'

'Of course we do, Jan,' Nicola said.

'Of course we do,' Donna echoed, a shade too brightly.

* * *

Gill was in a public call box. He had punched in a London number and now he waited, staring through the glass, seeing nothing. The ringing tone stopped as the 'phone at the other end was picked up.

'Julie? It's me.'

There was a silence for a couple of seconds. 'How are you, Gill?' she asked, a little cautiously.

'I'm fine,' he said, without thinking. 'No – no, I'm not fine. I'm lousy.'

'Why, what's happened?'

'Everything.' He heard the alien hollowness of his voice. Pressure was changing him, he reckoned. Soon he wouldn't know himself. 'You name it, it's happened.'

Julie said she was very sorry to hear it. She asked if the problem was with his job.

'Yeah, I've got the boot. But that's the least of it.'

He poured it all out to her, about taking the car, about joy-riding in it and knocking a man down, about trying to cover the evidence, then losing his job and winding up being blackmailed.

'Julie, you're my last hope. You've got to let me come and see you.'

She was quiet for a moment. 'I can't do anything, Gill,' she said at last. 'The only person who can help you is you.'

'Oh, don't give me that . . .'

'If you run away now,' she told him, 'you'll be running for the rest of your life.'

He was wishing he had never made this call. 'So what do you want us to do instead? Chuck myself off the blimmin' bridge?'

'I think you should give yourself up,' Julie said.

'Oh great!'

'I mean it, Gill. It's your only chance. Get it over with, then you can make a fresh start.'

Gill took a long steadying breath.

'Thank you,' he said. 'Thank you very much, duchess. I always knew, when the chips were down, I could count on you.'

He slammed down the 'phone.

* * *

In the main room at the Grove they were reliving the sweet destruction of Denton Burn's self-esteem.

'That was one killer moment, man,' PJ said. 'Hell's going to freeze over before Denton Burn take the mick out of *us* again.'

'Yeah,' Speedy said, grinning. 'I vote three cheers for Gazza! Hip, hip . . .'

The cheering rattled the windows. When it died down Geoff made a special announcement.

'While you're cheering,' he said, 'we've got something else to celebrate. Alison and Brad have just got engaged.'

More cheering broke out, much to the embarrassed pleasure of Alison and Brad. They found themselves surrounded; they had to answer questions from the kids about when the wedding would be, where the reception would be held and just who would be bridesmaids.

Across the room, Nicola was telling Debbie that Charlie was over the moon now Robert was back. Debbie, gazing at PJ, said she was glad Robert was back, too.

Gwen came in and told Nicola she was wanted on the 'phone in the office.

'Who is it?'

'Didn't say. But it's a him and he's in a call box.'

Nicola hurried out.

'It'll be that Paul,' Debbie said. 'She's dead stuck on him. I think he's a bit boring. Not like PJ.'

In the office Nicola snatched up the receiver. 'Hello?'

'Nicola? It's Jan. Listen, I'm at the ferry terminal. Kirsten is here.'

'Oh, Jan, I'm so pleased. Where has she been? Is she all right?'

'She went to London,' Jan said. 'No, she is not all right. Nicola, please – I need your help.'

* * *

Winston had seen Kelly leaving the main room and he followed her out. At the door he caught up with her.

'I thought you weren't speaking to us,' she said.

'I've got to know, man . . .'

'Go away,' she said. 'Please.'

'I saw you talking to Godzilla again. At the ground.'

'So?'

'So *why*? Why would you even have anything to do with rubbish like him? Why did you grass on us to him? I don't get it.'

'I didn't tell him! Cross my heart, hope to die – honest. I haven't told a soul, not a living –' Kelly stopped suddenly, looking shocked. 'My diary!' she said.

'What?'

'He must have nicked my diary. I couldn't find it yesterday. He did it before. I'll kill him, I will.'

'You wrote it in your diary? What a stupid . . .' Winston stopped. He frowned at Kelly. 'What do you mean, he did it before? How long have you known him?'

'Always. He's my brother.'

'Your *what*?'

'Carl. Godzilla. He's my brother. Oh Winston . . .' Kelly sighed. 'I was dead ashamed. I never wanted anyone to know.'

'I'll bet you blimmin' didn't,' Winston said bitterly.

He had always been trouble, Kelly said, even when the family had lived in the country. Their father had hoped that when they came to Newcastle Carl would get a proper job and settle down. But it hadn't worked out that way.

'Why *is* he like that?' Winston asked.

'I think he's scared if he starts acting normal, people won't notice him. I feel sorry for him.'

'And I feel sorry for you,' Winston said, truthfully.

'You won't tell anybody?' Kelly said.

'Not if you don't want me to.'

'And we're friends again?'

'Friends,' Winston said, smiling.

Inside, in the main room, Donna was looking for Nicola. Nobody seemed to know where she was. All Donna knew was that she had disappeared after the telephone call.

'I saw her going out,' Spuggie said.

'Where to?'

'How do I know?'

'Because you usually know everything,' Donna snapped.

At that moment, over at the ferry terminal, Jan was explaining to Nicola how he had told Kirsten, over and over, that he had never made love with Donna. Kirsten, however, still wouldn't believe him.

'It's true, Kirsten,' Nicola said. 'They didn't.'

'How would you know that?' Kirsten asked stiffly. 'You weren't there.'

'I know because she told me what happened. After she got back. She said she wanted to, but Jan wouldn't.'

Kirsten looked puzzled. 'He *wouldn't*?'

'No,' Nicola said. 'He said she was too young, and it wouldn't be right. She was dead miffed about it.'

'He gave her an engagement ring,' Kirsten said huffily.

'It was just a bit of costume jewellery, she asked him to buy it for her. It was Donna's idea to call it an engagement ring. Just one of her fantasies.'

'It is true, Kirsten,' Jan said.

All at once Kirsten seemed to melt. She let out a deep sigh.

'So it was all lies,' she said. 'Everything she told me. About you loving her, and coming back to me on the rebound . . .'

Nicola and Jan both nodded.

'But why?' Kirsten said. 'I thought we were friends. Why would she do such a wicked, terrible thing?'

'Because she's Donna,' Nicola said.

'Come, Kirsten.' Jan took her hand. 'The boat is ready to sail. We must go.'

He turned to Nicola and thanked her warmly.

'I was glad to help,' she said.

Jan and Kirsten went up the gang plank hand in hand. At the top they kissed, then turned and waved to Nicola. She waved back, tears blurring her eyes as she watched them go on board.

* * *

To get the evening's event in the main room going with a bang, Charlie had sung her song and the applause afterwards was deafening.

'So who is Maddie Brown, anyway?' PJ said to her. 'I bet your version beats her into a cocked hat.'

Charlie kissed him. For a moment they looked at each other.

'If ever Hopalong gives you the elbow,' PJ said, 'you know where to find me, superstar.' He turned away and tapped Debbie on the shoulder. 'Come on, then,' he said, 'let's you and me strut our stuff.'

Debbie grinned hugely as PJ whirled her on to the dance floor. Charlie went to the corner where Robert had parked his wheelchair.

'It made me so proud,' he told her, 'just watching you.'

She told him not to get hooked on it – that had been the very last time. She would never sing that song again, or any other for that matter.

'Rubbish,' Robert said.

'It's not,' she insisted. 'I've had show business – up to here.'

Out on the dance floor the music was loud and fast

and everybody was having a ball. At the height of it, as even Geoff and Gwen were getting drawn into the rhythm, Nicola stormed into the room. She came right on to the dance floor, caught Donna by the shoulder and slapped her hard across the face.

'You *bitch*!' Nicola hissed.

Donna stared at her. 'What was that for?'

'I never want to speak to you again as long as I live!'

Nicola stormed out again. Everybody stared at Donna.

'Come on kids,' PJ said, clapping his hands. 'This is supposed to be a celebration. Let's party party!'

The music was turned up louder. They all began to dance again.

All except Donna. She stood staring at the door, touching her cheek, looking very close to tears.

* * *

Out on the street, fretting about his predicament and wondering how Gill was, little Winston found himself staring at a headline on the side of a newspaper van. As it rounded the corner out of sight he couldn't quite believe what he had seen. He looked along the road and began running towards what he thought was a news-agent's. When he got there it turned out to be a travel shop.

He turned and nearly bumped into a paperboy pushing his bike along the pavement. Without hestitating Winston snatched a newspaper from the bag on the boy's shoulder. He stared at the front page. There it was, clear as day. HIT AND RUN DRIVER ARRES-TED. He read on, the words dancing before his eyes. It was the same accident all right. The man had been caught after forensic tests proved his car was the one involved in the incident.

Winston felt the grin spread across his face.

'Gill!' he whispered gleefully. 'It wasn't us, Gill! We're OK!'

He began running, heading for Gill's place. The paperboy shouted after him. Winston fished in his pocket, found a coin and threw it. The paperboy caught it and stared as Winston galloped off down the road.

'Papers don't cost a quid,' he murmured.

* * *

Gill lay on his bed, trembling with self-pity and mounting anger. He could scarcely believe what had happened to him. But it had happened, there was no undoing it. Every recent memory seemed to hurt, but what hurt most was the way Julie had cold-shouldered him. She had no right, he thought; it was nothing less than cruelty. She couldn't simply wash her hands of him like that. Not now, *especially* not now when he needed her and had no one else to turn to.

Tears welled as he thought of the way she had tried to get him to turn himself in. Did she think he was crazy, on top of everything else?

No, she didn't think he was crazy, because she didn't care enough to think about him at all. It had been obvious on the 'phone, the coolness, the disdain. She could hardly wait to get him off the line.

He sat up suddenly, fists clenched.

'If she thinks she can ditch me,' he hissed, 'she can think again!'

He got off the bed and stamped across the room. He found a sports bag and stuffed clothes into it.

'She'll never be rid of me!'

As he left the room Carl appeared.

'Haven't you forgotten something?' he said.

Gill's fist caught him on the bridge of the nose and he went sprawling. Gill strode out of the house. He had been gone less than a minute when Winston came running to the back door, clutching the newspaper.

'Don't bother,' Carl said, blood dripping from his nose. He grabbed Winston. 'He's gone. By the time you do find him, the cops'll be looking for the pair of you. Do you get what I mean?'

Winston jerked free.

'Buy a paper and get someone to read it to you, thicko,' he said, moving off again. 'And by the way, your sister knows who nicked her diary. I wouldn't bother mopping up too much.'

* * *

At weekends guards with dogs patrolled the compound at Fletcher's Garage. In Gill's present mood that presented no obstacle to his plans. He watched and waited and when he was sure the patrol was on the other side of the main building, he climbed the wall and dropped down into the yard. He opened one of the big gates and raced across to the showroom.

There were plenty of cars to choose from. He wanted something fast and not too conspicuous. After a couple of minutes he found one that was perfect. He checked the registration number, went to the office and forced the lock on the flimsy door. He crept inside. It didn't take long to find the right keys.

He went back to the car, threw his bag into the rear seat and slid in behind the steering wheel. With the key in the ignition he was about to turn on the engine when there was a roar from outside and a huge hairy guard dog hurled itself on to the bonnet. It barked furiously through the windscreen at Gill. For a moment he was paralysed, but as the animal slid off the bonnet, still barking, his reflexes came back. He switched on the engine, threw it in gear and drove out into the yard. The gate he opened earlier had swung partly shut but he was still able to drive through. He swung the steering wheel skilfully, straightening out and speeding along the road.

Approaching a corner he saw a familiar figure. It was Winston. He stopped, recognising Gill as he sped past. Gill watched in the mirror as Winston waved his newspaper.

'Can't stop, little buddy. . . .'

Gill's eyes were off the road for less than two seconds. When he looked again he was five metres away from a lorry. His foot didn't make it to the brake before they collided. The impact was like an explosion. For what seemed an age, pieces of glass and metal chinked and clattered on to the road.

After a long, horrified minute Winston began walking towards the crash. His legs were weak, hardly able to carry him. He didn't want to look at the wreckage, but he couldn't stop himself. As he got closer he began to tremble, terrified of what he might see.